THE SECRETS
WE KEEP

ALSO BY DANDELION REVOLUTION PRESS

Not Quite As You Were Told

THE SECRETS WE KEEP

PAIGE BASELICE

SAMANTHA BENTON

MARK BRUCE

ASHINI J. DESAI

KALYANI DESHPANDE

HAYLEY E. FRERICHS

PAIGE GARDNER

CATIE JARVIS

JAMES P. W. MARTIN

NATALIE MONAGHAN MUNROE

ADAM J. NEWTON

SARENA TIEN

KERRY TRAUTMAN

ALISA UNGAR-SARGON

SCARLET WYVERN

A Dandelion Revolution Press Publication

First published by Dandelion Revolution Press

Copyright © 2021 by Dandelion Revolution Press
All rights reserved.
ISBN: 978-1-0879-5145-4

This novel is entirely a work of fiction. The names, characters and incidents portrayed in it are the work of the author's imagination. Any resemblance to actual persons, living or dead, events or localities is entirely coincidental.

Dandelion Revolution Press has no responsibility for the persistence or accuracy of URLs for external or third-party Internet Websites referred to in this publication and does not guarantee that any content on such Websites is, or will remain, accurate or appropriate.

Cover art by Malik Awuah and Natalie Awuah of Elephants & Trains
Cover design by Dandelion Revolution Press
Typography by Hayley E. Frerichs

Dandelion Revolution Press
P.O. Box 215
Sellersville, PA. 18960
www.dandelionrevolutionpress.com

✦

First edition

To all who hold secrets within themselves—
and who find the power to set them free.

CONTENTS

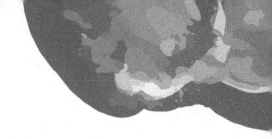

*Content notes included. Story may contain sensitive or triggering topics.

Sometimes we have something to hide.

1

A Mother's Curse

I hear you, Magic. I listen to you crackle through my bones, warning me my plan is folly. Warning me to set aside this madness. You always sound just like her, like the Queen of the Folk who bound us long ago. Do you remember, my Magic? When I asked the queen's favor and she granted me you? I know you do. You were around for the birth of the world, and you do not forget, though you beg me to. Alas, I will not set aside my mission. Not at your behest, nor mine. It is futile, mayhap. But futility is no excuse not to try.

Hush, Magic, hush. The rush of pain! My blood is screaming, such pain! You think I cannot bear it. Have I not borne worse in your presence? Not since my greatest sin have you fought so hard against my will. You were right then, Magic. You are wrong now. I must destroy the evil I have wrought. Too long there has been blood in the streets. Too long!

❖ ❖ ❖

The tea tray shakes in my grasp as I descend the cellar stairs, the sound of porcelain clinking together tinkling in my ears as the cups rattle against their saucers. The scent of stale perspiration mixed with the metallic tang of blood greets me as I reach the last step. The smell grows stronger as I make my way to the emaciated figure leaning against the wall. The irons dig into his wrists despite his weight loss. I set the tray down and hold one of the cups up to his lips.

"Drink," I say.

He lifts his head to look at me. The suspicion in his eyes is palpable, but he parts his lips obediently. I tilt the cup and he takes a few sips. Tea dribbles down his chin as I set down the cup and settle on the floor across from him.

"How long have I held you here, my friend?" I ask before taking a sip of my own tea, relishing the bitter taste.

The man stares at me blankly. There was a time he would have snapped at me, pulled against his irons until he was bloody and raw. But his fighting spirit shriveled away long ago.

"Years, decades perhaps. Time blends together," I muse.

He turns his head as if trying to tune me out, exposing the faded scar on his neck.

"You'll want to hear this," I say, grasping his chin and forcing him to look at me. "Because I'm going to tell you everything and then I will set you free."

◆ ◆ ◆

I should never have stridden into the Forbidden Wood. Every suckling babe knows not to make a deal with the Fair Folk. The children of Ireland are raised on mother's milk and cautionary tales of the fae. Above all else, one should never travel to the Kingdom Under the Hill. But I was ever desperate and folly bound.

Creatures from the Kingdom Under the Hill oft steal into our world, wolves the size of mountains, birds with breath of lightning and worse. Few survive an attack from such beasts. Dually, fae beasts can't survive long in our world, so it's best to just stay out of the Wood.

But as fierce as the fae are, there have always been tales of the wonders a faery might bestow on one found worthy. As a small child, I was fascinated with tales of the Fair Folk, though I was smart enough to have a healthy fear of them. I may never have gathered the courage to enter the Forbidden Wood had it not been for the plague that swept through my village in my seventeenth year.

Bodies were piled in the streets, the scent of burning flesh lingering in the air from the constant disposing of corpses. Children were kept locked up in their homes and the slightest cough raised suspicion. Then came the day my elder brother came home from tilling the fields, his eyes glassy, flecks of blood dusting his chin. My father took one look at him and told him to leave.

"No! He will die if we do nothing," I pleaded.

My father slammed the door shut and latched it, locking my brother out. "There is nothing to be done," he said faintly, staring at the locked door.

"You know that is not true."

He turned toward me, studying me with grave eyes. "There is nothing that can help us in that Wood."

I waited until my family slept before creeping out of our cramped cottage, the moon ripe in the sky by the time I reached the Forbidden Wood. The silhouettes of the trees in the darkness seemed sharp, almost wicked, and I nearly turned back more than once.

But my belief won out over my fear, and I soon reached the fabled clearing. In its center, a small hill radiated with ancient power. Taking a shuddering breath, I began to circle counterclockwise around the hill.

"Circle once to wake them. Twice to entice. To open the doorway, circle thrice." The old nursery rhyme floated through my head as I made my spherical journey. As my third lap ended, the hill transformed before my eyes into a pathway descending steadily underground.

"But be warned against this tide. Circle once not, nor circle twice, and never ever circle thrice." A nervous shiver tingled down my spine as I walked into the Kingdom Under the Hill.

The Kingdom Under the Hill wasn't like the world above. The air itself was heavy with Magic, the feel of it near suffocating as it pressed against my skin. I followed the pathway, trailing my fingers against the dirt walls. Despite being deep beneath the ground, the passage never darkened—illuminated, it seemed, by the air itself. The tunnel ended abruptly, and I found myself in what appeared to be an outdoor throne room.

Rowan trees lined a dais made of sparkling emerald on which sat a throne made of branches. Curled up like a cat in her oversized throne, her yellow-green eyes watchful, was the Fae Queen herself.

"Think once, think twice, and know your rights before you dare to speak. Lest you lose more than you seek to claim and wallow in defeat. Lest you come to regret the day we met, and the bargain struck between." She had a strange feline lilt to her voice. I found myself speechless before her.

3

"You do come to make a deal, do you not?" she said, jumping down from her throne to stand before me. She was a small thing, three feet in height with pitch black hair down to her ankles, yet for her stature and youthful appearance there was an aura of ancient wisdom to her being.

"I wish to be a powerful witch, so that I might heal the sick."

The queen tilted her head to the side as if in judgment.

"How very noble of you. Though noble is so very dull. Mortals are like flowers, blooming brightly only to wilt away. Healing them won't change that. Why not ask for something more fulfilling?"

I felt a flash of anger at her harsh words. "A plague has reached my village. My brother has it. To heal him, to spare others pain, there is nothing that would fulfill me more."

"And yet, do you ask for the health of your people? Do you ask that I heal your brother? No, you ask for power." Her eyes gleamed with amusement as my face heated in embarrassment, for I had not thought to ask such things, yet I held her gaze. I opened my mouth to speak but she waved a hand at me dismissively.

"No matter. I shall grant your wish should you agree to tarry for a day and a night in my kingdom."

How naïve I was to think I could bargain with the fae and not be burned. A day and a night? Though I was anxious to get home, I thought a day and a night in the Kingdom Under the Hill was more than worth my brother's life. "I agree to your terms."

The queen raised her brows, smiling with delight. "Then the deal is struck."

She snapped her fingers and I felt the Magic meld into my bones. *I felt you latch onto my soul and my soul opened wide to embrace you as a part of it.*

For a day and a night, I danced among faeries and imps. I drank enchanted wine and chased will-o-the-wisps, all the while glowing as the Magic raced through my veins—as it came to know me, to love me.

My bargain fulfilled, I wearily returned from the Kingdom Under the Hill. Tired but determined, I quickly made my way home. Perhaps had I been less exhausted I would have noticed how worn our cottage looked, or how the fields which had been barren when I left were now rife with cabbage. Alas, it wasn't until I opened the front door and saw strangers staring at me with suspicion, that I realized anything was amiss.

Fifty years had passed while I was under the hill, along with my family and everyone I knew.

◆ ◆ ◆

Several years later, I gave birth to my Phalen. By the time he came into the world, I was well known for my healing abilities. People from villages near and far would travel to my home in hopes of being cured. And I never failed once. Not until Phalen.

Phalen, my sweet boy with hair of fire and sea-kissed eyes. Oh, how I doted on him—my curious, rebellious boy.

Phalen was born with an adventurous spirit, and as the years passed, he began to resent me for my overprotectiveness. I should have allowed him to fight with the other lads in town, should have let him get into mischief. But I had lost so much, I couldn't risk losing Phalen as well. Perhaps had I not been so protective, he would not have run off to prove himself. But I smothered him and off he ran. Straight into the Forbidden Wood.

Phalen heard the same rumors we all did that summer—a terrible beast stalked the Forbidden Wood and no man that crossed its path had yet survived. Some of the foolhardier men in our village planned to gain glory by slaying the beast, and my Phalen wanted to fight with them. He was fourteen and aching to prove himself.

"We must not trifle with a creature from the Kingdom Under the Hill. The Fair Folk will call it home soon enough if it doesn't die first. No need to die fighting a futile battle," I told him as I set two bowls of oatmeal on the table.

"Mother, beasts like this cannot be allowed to exist in our woods. We must defend ourselves," Phalen said, slamming his fist down hard enough to make the bowls shake.

"It is not our wood," I drawled. "It is the Forbidden Wood for a reason. You cannot win a fight against a fae creature."

"I won't be fighting alone. The bravest men in the village will be at my side."

"You won't be fighting at all, Phalen. Those men are fools. If they face that beast, they will die. And you will not be with them. I'll hear no more about it."

Phalen glowered at me as we ate in silence. Though he was unusually quiet throughout the day, I thought the matter resolved. I awoke in the morning to find my son's bed empty. He had left with the village men in the night to fight the beast.

I ran into the woods, fear and fury working in tandem inside me. Deeper and deeper into the woods I ran, ignoring the foreboding feeling forming in my stomach. Phalen, I had to find my Phalen before the beast did. In desperation, I sent my Magic out in all directions to find a trail of his scent. I crouched, catching my breath until I felt my Magic tug against my soul, leading me to my son.

I smelled the carnage before I heard it—blood and feces and fear. A deafening growl that reverberated through my bones, that made my Magic shiver in my veins. I ran towards the sound even as my Magic urged me not to do so.

Breaking through a copse of trees, I saw it. The beast was the size of my cottage, lo a giant wolf with yellow-green eyes reminiscent of the Fae Queen's. From its fangs dripped a dark venom, leaving smoking holes in the ground where it fell. I saw the creature snarl as Phalen leapt between the bodies of his fallen comrades, armed with only a small dagger. He lunged. The beast swiped its great claws across his chest; I felt the blow as if it had struck me instead. Phalen did not get up.

I gathered my strength, my Magic pulsing under my skin, fueling it with my rage and despair. The creature snarled, rushing towards me. I unleashed my power upon it, the malignant green light that sparked from my fingertips carving through the creature's chest. It stared at me dumbfounded as its eyes glazed over, then collapsed to the forest floor. I turned, rushing past the corpses littering the ground, and knelt beside Phalen as he convulsed. His breathing was ragged and his skin ashen. Green puss wept from the gashes in his shredded open chest and the exposed tissue was turning a putrid brown. My boy, my sweet Phalen.

I pushed both myself and my Magic to our limits that night. But the wound wouldn't heal. I recited every prayer, cast every blessing, every spell. None had any effect. *I should have let him die.* Fourteen. He was barely grown. With each failed cure his skin grew paler, his breathing more ragged. It was not within my power, our power. *Magic, do you remember my desperation?* I was a fool, but I was a fool out of love for my child. I should never have returned to the queen. I should never have struck a second bargain. *I should have let him die.*

I would not lose Phalen, I would not. And so, I kissed his cheek and left him lying in the woods by the beast's corpse as I hurriedly made my way to the Kingdom Under the Hill.

I circled counterclockwise thrice around the hill as quick as I dared. As soon as the hill opened, I ran down the path. I emerged directly in the court of the Fae Queen as if she had been expecting me.

Twenty years since I'd last seen her, though she looked not a breath older. Looking at her, I became conscious of my mortal skin, the age lines and blemishes I had acquired since my last visit. My hair flecked with grey, my beauty faded. The queen purred. Those who haven't dealt with the Fair Folk directly never realize how similar they can be to cats. Not in appearance but in mannerisms. They hiss and preen. Quick-footed and even quicker of tongue. It's a fool's errand bargaining with the fae. A deal with the devil himself may yet be safer. But I suppose my love for Phalen made me a fool.

"You return to me. I did not think to see you again, mortal."

"I had not thought to return, but necessity demands it," I answered. My words were cold, clipped.

The queen's lips spread in a wicked grin, exposing her sharp canines. "You have come to make another bargain."

"My son was gravely injured. I have cast every spell, every blessing upon him. But nothing has worked. I wish to heal him, and I mustn't tarry, not this time."

The queen pouted. "Your son lays dying because he attempted to slay one of my creatures, but you were the one who took my pet's life, are you not?" She eyed me up and down before nodding, as if my silence were answer enough. "I can offer you no spell to save him. The bargain cannot be struck."

I bowed my head in sorrow, clenching my fists at my sides.

"I can however offer you a curse, a curse that will spare his life if you would accept such a boon."

I felt my Magic, screaming in my veins, like wildfire trying to warn me, and I nearly doubled over. A fae bargain may come with barbs, but a gift from the fae is akin to being gifted a rose bush that turns out to be all thorns. I should have let him die—I should have refused her gift and sat with him as he passed—then mourned and buried him.

But I let my love damn us, didn't I, Magic? When I pass, it'll be Satan who passes my name between his lips. How strong is our bond I wonder? Will you be ripped from me when I pass on? It is selfish, but I hope not. With you in my veins, I can bear the worst tortures of hell.

"My queen, I would be honored to accept such a boon." The words came out strained as my Magic thrashed inside my throat. The Fae Queen smiled ferally and produced a wooden dagger which she used to cut her palm, smearing the blade with her blood. Handing me the dagger, she whispered in my ear what I must do.

Phalen's breath was so weak when I returned that I thought he was already dead. His usually fair skin had turned a mottled gray. I stood frozen, staring down at his limp form, sure I'd taken too long, certain he was dead. Was that why the queen had given me the curse? As a morbid joke, knowing I would be too late? But no, I saw his chest rise ever so slightly. Oh, how I wish I had returned too late.

I knelt beside Phalen and my Magic surged against my control, begging me to stop, but I held it tightly within the trappings of my soul, and harnessing our power, I chanted the curse the queen had gifted to my lips. *I should have listened to you, my Magic.*

I crawled over to the beast's corpse, every movement a struggle as my Magic fought against me. I took the wooden dagger the queen had dampened with her blood, chanting under my breath as I stuck the dagger deep into the monster's chest, letting its blood meld with that of the queen. Struggling, my breath short, I crawled back to Phalen. My Magic sent a searing pain down my thighs, and my legs gave out beneath me. Determined, I pulled myself by the elbows until I sat awkwardly at my son's side. I looked down at my sweet boy, my Phalen, and swiftly struck the blood-stained wooden dagger into the wound in his chest. Then I waited.

Just before dawn, he opened his eyes.

Phalen was on his feet within the hour. We walked arm in arm through the Forbidden Wood, back to our cottage, Phalen occasionally rubbing a gentle hand across his chest in wonder. We arrived home with the sun still waking in the sky. Phalen had an energy to him I had not seen before, but I was far too weary to be suspicious of it. I lay upon my bed and let sleep take me, ignoring the sour feeling in my gut.

✦ ✦ ✦

I would never have believed Phalen had been on his deathbed only days before had I not seen it with my own eyes. He seemed to be in perfect physical health. Muscles bulged from his once gangly arms and his appetite could not be sated no matter how much food I set before him.

As the weeks passed, Phalen grew sullen and withdrawn, though there was a restlessness to him. When he wasn't eating, he was silent and brooding. I tried to ignore these changes in his behavior. I tried to forget the curse.

Then came the night my Magic pulled against my skin, urging me to wake. A knot of dread settled in my stomach as I threw on my slippers and allowed my Magic to guide me out into the night. Bathed in the light of a full moon, I walked around to the back of the cottage and through the fields, my Magic tugging me along, until I reached the edge of the Forbidden Wood. I looked around impatiently, wondering why my Magic had compelled me out of bed, when I heard a grotesque wet, crunching noise. I turned slowly, the hairs on my neck raising.

Hunched over the body of a young man was a monster. It opened its maw, exposing sharp, blood-stained canines then ripped a chunk of flesh from the dead man's stomach. Coarse auburn fur covered its crouched form, its head like that of a wolf. I stepped backward, pulling my Magic close around me. A branch snapped beneath my feet and the creature stilled. The wolf-man looked up at me with sea-kissed eyes.

"Mother." It spoke with Phalen's voice but there was a dark edge to it now. "Go home. I will return before the moon sets."

"Phalen," I pleaded, my voice shaking. I took a step towards him. "Stop this. We can stop this. I'll find a cure."

"Go home," Phalen growled.

So, this was what I had cursed him to be in my desperation. Not waiting to see if I heeded his order, Phalen turned back to the man's corpse—to his meal. As I shakily walked back to the cottage, I swear I heard the Fae Queen's tinkling laughter. I did not sleep that night. *I should have let him die.*

The next night when my Magic tugged against me, urging me to wake, I refused. I lay stiffly in my bed, eyes squeezed shut until the sun's rays danced across my eyelids. A few days later, I heard that the body of a young woman was found on a neighboring farm, mutilated as if wolves had been feasting on her.

Phalen grew more withdrawn, more restless by the day. He knew I had cursed him, but instead of horror at what I had done, he showed only apathy. His hunger grew even more insatiable, and I found it hard to keep enough food on the table. I dreaded every night, afraid he would again become the beast. I still remember the sound of bone crunching between his teeth as I walked home that night—away from Phalen and what I'd done to him. He did not transform again and after several weeks I let myself believe it was done with. I was a fool.

◆ ◆ ◆

I awoke to my Magic pulling against my insides so violently that I leaned over the side of the bed, heaving. Clutching my stomach, I gasped for breath. I heard a deep growl echo through the trees followed by the screams. I ran. I'm uncertain I even knew where I was running to until I found myself in the village square.

Bodies decorated the streets, broken at odd angles, some missing limbs, some with bites taken out of their throats or stomachs. Bile rose in my throat as the coppery stench of blood filled my nostrils. I let out a sharp sob and heard a guttural growl in response. Phalen came toward me at a run, his snout dripping with stranger's blood and his eyes a storm at sea. I braced myself for impact, closing my eyes. So, this is how it will end, I thought. The fear coursing through my veins was not merely my own—my Magic shivered with terror.

I felt his warm breath against my face. The smell made me gag. I opened my eyes. Phalen stood before me, his jaw twitching.

"Go home, mother," he snarled. Human innards snagged between his wicked teeth.

I did not go home. I scoured every cottage, every stable, in a desperate search for survivors. But Phalen, my once gentle boy, was as thorough as he was ruthless. And for the first time, I thought I should have let my boy die.

It was several weeks later that Phalen moved from our cottage, building himself a small home in the heart of the Forbidden Wood. He saw the way I looked at him, a mixture of fear and regret. Leaving may have been the last kind thing he ever did for anyone.

◆ ◆ ◆

Still, once a month, on the first quarter moon, I make the trek into the wood to sup with my son. Every full moon, my Phalen turns into a hideous beast. Every moon, he loses more of his soul. I do not know if any of my beloved Phalen still resides within that cursed body.

Many a year I have searched for a cure. Many a year more I have searched for a way to destroy this beast I've created. Phalen hungers as much for violence as he does meat. How many ruined villages have I walked with soil stained red by the blood Phalen has spilt? How many graves have I dug, bodies have I buried? The worst is when he lets his victims live, forcing families to choose between killing their loved one out of mercy or watching as they shift into a creature like my son.

It was two of these surviving victims that I bound, one in the cellar, one in the attic.

"I have tortured you both brutally and without remorse for years," I say. The man shrugs in his irons, otherwise silent. "You poor creatures. I have cast thousands of spells, curses, and incantations over the years. Finally, I have found it. I have found a way to set you free. A blessed dagger made of Rowan wood inserted into the site of the original wound." The man stares at the ground blankly. "Your brother in the attic is at rest. It is time I set you free as well."

The broken creature before me whimpers as I pull the dagger of Rowan out from where I'd tucked it against my leg. I hold the dagger level with his throat where Phalen bit him long ago. "Please," he chokes out.

My hand trembles as I thrust the dagger into his throat. He slumps backward, his head smacking against the cellar wall.

Sliding the dagger out of the puncture wound, I tuck it back into the sheath wrapped around my thigh. I place our empty teacups on the tray and use my hand to push up off the ground, balancing the tray between my elbow and hip.

It's just us now, my Magic.

I can only hope Phalen will not guess at my intentions, that he will not notice the bulge of the dagger against my thigh. For, finally, I have gathered the strength to end Phalen's cursed existence. Finally, I have found a way to lay my boy to rest.

✧ ✧ ✧

Scarlet Wyvern is part poet, part girl, and part dragon. Since she was a young hatchling Scarlet has reveled in the written word. Wyvern is fascinated by mythology, especially that which concerns the fair folk and is utterly obsessed with the original Grimm fairy tales. When she is not busy writing or soaring through the sky lighting villages on fire, Wyvern delights in reading, photography, playing video games, singing karaoke and making snarky comments while sipping the blood of her enemies out of a crystal chalice. To learn more visit ScarletWyvern.com or follow @ScarletWyvern on Twitter.

2

Why We Collided

The biggest mistake of my life was dating a man.

Put those meninism signs down. I'm not saying that all men suck, even though under the umbrella of the patriarchy, technically they're all awful. But I liked August and his sunshine smile well enough. He was all words and art and color like the spine of a book, the kind of guy who you wanted to breathe in and read cover to cover.

When I'd taken him home, my parents had half-joked about wanting me to marry him, making sure to do it in Mandarin so August couldn't understand. He'd glanced at me, confusion clear in his amber eyes. I'd patted his knee and opened my mouth to tell him the truth, but one of my cousins patted his shoulder and laughed a lie. "They said you're too pretty for her!"

August's confusion spread from his eyes to his face. People looked at him and thought danger, not beauty, because society had made his skin color a crime. Once he'd tried to help a lost child find his parents, and store security accused him of attempted kidnapping until I emerged from the bathroom, drunk in the situation, and yelled at the guard, making sure to throw in a few random words in Mandarin for good measure. People fear foreign, and Mandarin was as foreign as I could get.

For me, foreign was the familiar. When I was younger, I'd wilted beneath the weight of two cultures, but now I welcomed the weight and wore it like a wish. Perhaps that was why I'd felt so at home in August's house—two different languages infusing the air, mingling sweetly with the scent of distinctly un-American food. When his Haitian mother whispered, *"Yo ta dwe marye,"* to his Senegalese father who murmured something back in Wolof, I didn't ask what they'd said because they reminded me of why August and I collided in orbit. We were both trilingual, first-generation kids at a college that was so white, everyone assumed we were international students.

But a secret hung between us, and when untold, a secret seeps into the veins of a relationship, poisoning it from the inside out.

I think both of us suspected. But neither of us wanted to breathe life into the words lest they become truth. So, they simmered unspoken, alive only in denial, until finally, the secret settled over us like dust. Eventually, inevitably, someone disturbed the secret, stirring motes and letters and syllables all around us. The inadvertent culprit turned out to be my parents when they repeated in front of August that we should get married, murmuring, *"Tāmen yīnggāi jiéhūn."*

That evening, instead of driving us home, August swerved into the park where we'd had our first date. He gave only ambiguous answers to my questions until we reached a bench half-hidden by flowering fuchsias.

I rescued a bumblebee from the dirt, cradling it next to a flower. "August, what are we doing?" I asked, waiting until the bee climbed aboard before turning around.

He sank to one knee. "Lyra, *nǐ yuàn yì jià gěi wǒ mā?*"

I looked at him blankly, unable to reply for two reasons. One, his Mandarin had been the flawless rise and fall of an ocean rather than the jarring, discordant bloodbath carried out by every non-Asian I'd ever met. Two, I loved August, and that was exactly why I couldn't marry him.

August misinterpreted my distress. "I didn't butcher the pronunciation, did I? I've only been learning Mandarin for six months."

"Marry you?" I repeated in response to his first question, as if he'd spoken in an unknown language and echoing his words could help me untangle their meaning.

His fingers furled around the ring I still hadn't picked up, would probably never pick up. His eyes darted down to his dashiki. "Maybe we should have this conversation on even ground."

August reached for the flare of my waist to draw me closer, but as usual, my hip bone sliced into his palm. Instead, he laced his fingers through mine, my electrician calluses rough against his gentle preschool teacher hands.

He needn't have bothered. I fell to my knees instantly. It was a miracle I'd managed to stay standing.

"Lyra—" His Adam's apple moved up, then down, but not another whisper of sound came out. The weed wedged in my throat had also lodged in his.

I tried to fill the silence for August. One dandelion seed escaped.

"I'm—" I said.

But then a dandelion seed drifted from his mouth. "—gay," he said.

We stared. Stared until the wind blew all the dandelion seeds away and the stems vaulted out of our vocal cords and we were forced to find our own words because the sunset had stolen them all.

"Hang on," I said at last. "Were you finishing my confession or making your own?"

"Both," he said. "I'm gay. Wait, you're gay?"

Laughter replaced the lump in my throat. "I'm gay."

August sat down. "Good thing I took those Mandarin lessons."

I sat down beside him. "You could've asked in any other language."

"Yeah," he agreed. "But then I wouldn't have fallen in love with my Chinese tutor."

As I plucked a wayward leaf from his shoulder, I wondered why his statement held the hint of a mystery waiting to be solved. My mouth dropped open. "No way. You took my cousin up on his offer?"

"I wanted to know what your parents were saying," August said. "Then mine said the same thing. And I thought..." He dangled the ring off a fingertip. "I don't know what I'd have done if you'd accepted."

"If I'd been straight?" I snorted at the impossibility that had nearly become a farcical possibility. The sound made August laugh so hard that he dropped the ring, and then both of us were nearly sobbing, and in that laughter, we let our socially constructed straight selves die. It was one of those rare instances where people go willingly to their deaths.

The greatest mistake of August's life, it turned out, had been dating a woman.

We'd each been the other's easy choice, but not the right one. Our romance had been the kind scripted for books, screens, and stages—for everyone but us.

And August, despite his summer namesake, couldn't compare to Monday's burnished beauty. Whereas August had merely existed within the patriarchy, neither supporter nor dissenter yet still guilty in his neutrality, Monday was wild with wanting to defy the patriarchy. She threw on crop tops and leggings and bright colors, clothing all deemed inappropriate and unprofessional for her body type, gloriously messy compared to August's neat Oxfords and guayaberas and dashikis.

I fell for her slowly and destructively, a star hurtling headfirst through the hellfire of heteronormativity. But this was the kind of explosion that wrought change instead of havoc, that birthed life instead of death. If August had been a book, the promise of a story, then Monday was a constellation—a sight that you never wanted to stop staring at, a shape and a myth that made you impatient for the day to end so that you could gaze into the night and find her again. Even her freckles looked like stars, a galaxy that I soon learned also dusted her shoulders and bloomed and burst across her back.

God, I'm so gay. I can't believe I let society tell me I should be straight.

✦ ✦ ✦

Monday roars with laughter. "You almost got married? To a gay man?"

"Shut up," I say, but my smile ruins my indignation. "Come on, we're going to be late."

"No! You have to tell me more!" Monday cries even as she follows me to the door. "What was his name?"

I fish the car keys out of her pocket. "I'll tell you if we survive my parents."

She sobers. "Are you sure you want to go?"

"No," I sigh, opening the front door anyways. "Facing them is about as appealing as attending a white civil rights rally."

We meet my parents at a Thai restaurant, neutral grounds where there are no ghosts of August and no memories of Monday. I was surprised they'd reached out. Like most people, they'd subscribed to the heteronormative narrative of marriage and children long ago and expected me to follow the same script.

The conversation goes in circles, repeating history. I don't know why I agreed to come. Hope, I suppose, and hope doesn't die easily.

Not like patience. Patience is easy to kill. I throw my hands up into its corpse. "Have you forgotten? He's marrying Jun."

My dad's mouth flattens at the mention of my cousin. "At least they get married."

I refrain from rolling my eyes. "Would you be happier if I married Monday?"

Neither of my parents respond. Monday coughs into her bubble tea.

Finally, my mom says, "August make you happy, too."

I think about it. August and I had followed the confines of an already mapped out empire, but Monday and I were a new world, forging our own queendom in territory never touched by man.

"No," I say at last. "He made me *think* I was happy."

Sarena Tien is a queer Chinese American feminist who is currently a PhD student of French Literature at Cornell University. Once upon a time, she used to be so shy that two teachers once argued whether she was a "low talker" or a "no talker." She's since learned how to scream, and her poetry and prose have appeared in online publications such as The Feminist Wire, Bustle, On She Goes, Entropy, Argot, Decoded Pride, and Sylvia. When she's not trying to become a polyglot, she can often be found crocheting cuddly creatures or folding far too many origami stars.

3

A FALSE START*

On our way to the abortion clinic, there is an old, boxy brown car, flipped and blocking one lane of traffic on the 405. The BMWs, the beat-up Nissans, and everything in-between snake around the Los Angeles highway curves and move in small increments, together, like a giant connected creature. The earthy, dead tree scent of the joint my boyfriend, Troy, and I shared the night before lingers in the car.

"See Kat, I told you we needed to leave extra early," he says, one hand on the wheel and the other gently squeezing my thigh.

"Yes, you're always proving yourself right," I reply. Even with traffic, we will arrive early for my appointment due to Troy's stronghold on time. *A good skill for a father to have.* The thought tightens my throat, but I won't let myself cry.

It's the year of the Rio Olympic Games—Michael Phelps is adding to his illustrious room of gold in a Scrooge McDuck-like fashion and the U.S. Women's Gymnastics Team, led by the superhuman Simone Biles, is about to fetch U.S.'s first back-to-back gymnastics championships. I decide that this is how I will remember this day, this time. I play the Olympic theme song over in my head to keep myself occupied—those proud trumpets, the brass fanfare. Despite my attempts at distraction, I keep putting my hands onto my belly as if anticipating the pain that will ensue later in the day. I feel bad for the damage, the confusion. *What the fuck?* My uterus will say. *What am I supposed to do now?* Or, *Damn, I've been literally waiting twenty years to try this shit out, and just when I thought I was going to have my shot...* Or maybe, actually, *Phew!*

*Content notes: abortion

That was about to be a shit ton of work and I was really not looking forward to it.

✦ ✦ ✦

The ultrasound woman is young and somber. She sticks a long, wide, and heavily lubricated pole into my vagina and searches around with it. A little square screen, resembling the old Macintosh released the year of my birth, 1984, sits next to me, facing away. This is the hard part.

"Do you have to pee?" the woman asks me.

"Well, I always have to pee," I tell her. "But I did just pee in a cup for you."

She laughs a little. "Your bladder is full," she tells me.

"Is that a problem?"

"No." She searches around for a moment more. "I can see the pregnancy," she says.

I like this way of putting it. It seems right. *The pregnancy.* It is nothing more than that. It is a thing not created, not formed, and not going to be.

"Five weeks and five days," she says.

Five is my favorite number. I wonder what this means. I took the number on as my favorite when I was five years old because I felt that at that age, I was old enough to think, reflect, and decide, but young enough to have everything taken care of for me. At five, I felt there was an ultimate sort of guided freedom, and I feared—correctly—that such a thing would be lost in the following years of life. If I decided to keep *the pregnancy*, I could have a five year old in no time. Something about this thought, something about the five weeks and five days, makes me start to cry.

"I feel sad and alone," I text Troy, who sits outside in the waiting room, so proximate but so far away.

"What can I do?" he texts back.

Get over your commitment issues? Stop pining over younger, bigger breasted girls on Instagram? Marry me? Be a partner that makes me feel ready to have a child? I want to reply, but I refrain.

The ultrasound woman leaves, and I think for a moment that nothing will be okay. I imagine that I'll soon be bawling on the floor,

19

inconsolable. I imagine that I'll go home to the small neat apartment by the ocean that I share with Troy, grab a few necessities, and straight up walk out on my whole life. Fortunately, a nurse practitioner, a Spanish-looking woman in her late forties, dressed in bright pink scrubs, comes in like a breath of fresh air.

"You are here at the perfect time," she tells me. "There is nothing yet, just cells. Five weeks will be easy to pass."

She pops the first pill out of its tin foil backing and places it in the palm of my hand with a glass of water.

"Take," she says. Asking no questions, passing no judgments. "This makes it stop. No more growing."

I swallow the pill and take a deep sigh. The nurse walks back over to the other side of the room to look at my chart. I feel relieved, elated. Everything is manageable. Everything is fine.

"You plan to have a child someday?" she asks.

I nod with assurance. In this moment, I feel sure. She scrolls through my chart and does a double take of it and then me.

"How old are you?" she asks.

"Thirty-one."

"No!" she says. She looks at the chart again. I don't think she is putting on an act, people are often taken aback about how I look much more like a girl of twenty-four than like a woman of thirty. It's even a bit alarming to me. Perhaps if I looked more my age, I'd be able to settle more easily into what is expected of me during this phase of my life. Would a bit more body fat, some forehead lines and eye creases encourage me to grow up, to be ready to have a child and live a more adult life?

"You do not look thirty," she says definitively. "What's your secret?"

"Yoga, I guess." After I say this, I feel like a Los Angeles cliché. *How did I turn into this? How did I get here? Twenty-one year old's have abortions, not thirty-one year old's. What has gone so wrong inside of me? Why am I so sure that I don't yet want a child?*

"Yoga. I need to try this," she says.

I nod, encouragingly.

The nurse explains the next set of pills to me. I will take them in 24 hours. I will let them sit in my cheek for a half hour until they dissolve.

That will cause my uterus lining to shed. That will cause me a considerable amount of pain for a few hours and maybe a few days and then it'll be over. It all seems rather precise. I didn't really know how it worked before today. I actually thought all abortions had to be surgical, even very early term. No one in my life has ever shared their experience of an abortion with me, at least not in any detail. As I sit in the clinic, on the sticky plastic pedestal, I'm saddened by this. I wonder who I will share this experience with. Will it become a secret that I need to hold, in fear of other's differing understandings and judgments?

"Okay," the nurse says, ready to dismiss me. "No tampons. No intercourse. No pools or oceans for two weeks."

"Oceans!" I exclaim. She looks surprised. Maybe no one in her office has ever exclaimed 'Oceans!' just after having an abortion induced.

"Yes, no oceans," she assures me. "Your cervix will be opened. We don't want any bacteria getting in there."

"I wish you had told me that before I swallowed this pill!" I suddenly feel shaky, visibly upset. I've been duped. Lied to. Led astray. "I'm going scuba diving this weekend. The trip is all set up and paid for. I finished my certification two weeks ago. I can't cancel!"

"Scuba diving?" she asks. "Isn't it scary under there?"

"A bit scary, but more so it's beautiful."

"Supposed to be no exerting yourself. No ocean," she reiterates. "Your cervix will be open."

I try to imagine it, my cervix, open like a gaping mouth at the dentist's. Or is it more subtle than that? Open like the little lips of a fish when you throw it some breadcrumbs in a pond. Perhaps if I try hard enough, I can will it to close.

"Is there anything I can do?" I ask, almost in tears yet again.

"Maybe pour some cement between your legs and don't let any water get in," she laughs, then shakes her head and smiles. She can see I've been spun into a tizzy. "It's okay," she says. "Go at your own risk. It will probably be fine."

The nurse folds up her papers. I watch the way her lips purse and her face creases at the corners as she goes about her tasks. It is clear that she has done this so many times. Her hair cascades in soft curls down her back that toss from side to side as she organizes and arranges her departure from the small room. In this moment, I love her the way I once loved my grandmother, fully and without judgment and knowing she would never harm me.

"Good luck and stay young," she tells me. "Yoga and scuba diving," she says with a nod, as if this is now her mission.

I will likely never see this woman again, but she has granted me two precious gifts: acceptance of my five week and five day abortion and permission to go scuba diving. As I enter back into the waiting room, I can tell my face looks more optimistic than Troy expected.

"Babe? All done?" he says. He kisses me twice on the lips, then takes my hand, as if I am his child, and leads me out towards the parking lot. That song pops into my head about the lime and the coconut, and I sing it quietly on the way to our car.

✦ ✦ ✦

From the clinic, we head to the pier at Hermosa Beach—we've both taken the day off work so why not enjoy it? We walk out on the pier and happen upon a Los Angeles lifeguard swimming competition. Perhaps they are doing it in honor of the Olympics, or more likely, it's something they do every summer. The lifeguards gallop into the water, unabashedly flailing arms in a rush to get in as fast as possible. They start a strenuous swim through the break and out to the other side where their strokes turn elegant and then eventually tired, as they round the red buoy markers.

There was a time that I wanted to be a lifeguard, not so that every surfer and tourist within a mile radius would drool over my bikini body, and not for the noble cause of potentially saving lives. I was drawn to the job because of the regiment. I would have liked to be forced to wake up early to jog on the beach, to swim in strenuous currents, to be always ready for the task of pulling a heavy struggling body into shore. I would have liked to spend my days outside, staring at the ocean with purpose.

A few of the contestants are nearing the shore. They ride the waves with aggressive kicks and run haphazardly out of the water and to the red finish line.

"We should do a triathlon someday," I say.

"We surf, we scuba dive, we hike. There's only time for so many things," Troy states.

I think of how a baby is one of the things we've decided we don't have time for.

The breeze on the pier is soft and cool and mixes with the sun to goose bump my arms in an almost complimentary way. I close my eyes and listen to the sounds of the waves crashing against the shore and imagine what it would feel like to dive in, that rush of cold and silence. Whenever I am near water, I want to be inside of it.

"Are we hungry?" my boyfriend asks. The coordinating of our eating is something that he hates about being in a relationship. That we always have to be hungry at the same time, interested in the same type of food; that we have to decide what to eat—together—is a burden he bears more heavily than a person ought to.

"Sure," I say. "Let's eat."

We sit in the shade at a restaurant near the pier on a small outdoor patio. Sitting beside us are three women in their sixties, maybe a little older than our parents, chatting about the Olympics as they share a bottle of some afternoon bubbly rosé.

"And that poor French sprinter," one woman says. She has short dark hair teased from a beauty parlor. She takes a sip of her drink and her lipstick leaves its pink print on the glass. "Just one flinch and his dreams of Olympic glory destroyed," she says. "What a heartbreak!"

"What do you think about that new rule?" her friend asks. She has long earrings made of Abalone or something equally iridescent. They dangle to almost meet with her slightly hunched and upraised shoulders.

"It's not fair!" the third woman says strongly. She is the one of the three who has most clearly had work done on her face. Maybe a lift and some collagen dispersed throughout. "It's not right!"

They are talking about Wilhem Belocian. They are talking about the false start rule initiated in 2010 that no longer gives racers one warning but instead enforces immediate disqualification if they literally jump the gun at the onset of a race.

23

"They are the top athletes in the world," Abalone Earrings says. "They must be held accountable. There is no room for error at this level of the game."

"Games!" Teased Hair exclaims. "The Olympics are just that, a game. We are not robots and we all err sometimes."

They are talking about the 110 meter hurdle on Monday night, just two days past. I'm not a track enthusiast, but as a former gymnast I mostly watch the Summer Olympics to view with envy and love my old passion. But on that Monday night my eyes had filled with tears as Belocian paced the track with his hands on his head after he realized what he had done. After all his training. One preemptive move and it was all over. He unzipped his deep blue and red costume, separating the letters FRA from the NCE across his chest. He crumpled to the ground.

At the time, I didn't find it particularly odd. Perhaps, in hindsight, I had been overly emotional due to the hormones pumping through my system unbeknownst to me. I have always had a special empathy for those moments where we so fully let ourselves down in this harsh and unforgiving world. When we do things that can never be undone.

"He'll lay in bed every night for the rest of his life regretting that moment," the third woman says, with her tightly pulled back cheeks that don't let on how much she feels. "We are too hard on ourselves," she continues. "I've learned that much."

I wonder how these women have come to know each other. How long they have lived in Los Angeles, how long they have all been friends. They must have each lived many different lives by now, phases of this human experience.

"I wonder what we'll be like at that age," I whisper to Troy.

"Old, babe. Old," he says. I can tell by the dullness in his green-grey eyes that he doesn't imagine us together at that age. He is not the grow-old-with-me type. What is a girl to do when she's thirty-one and in love with the type of man who can't speak of forever?

My rather large steak, tomato, and avocado baguette arrives like a challenge set out before me. "I'm going to do my best to eat the whole thing," I tell Troy. "Because I'm sure that I won't have an appetite later."

"Have at it!" As I reach for my sandwich, he intercepts my hand across the table and holds it. "I've got you," he says. And he does.

✦ ✦ ✦

When we get home to our one bedroom apartment in Santa Monica that we can barely afford, Troy sits with me while the pills turn chalky in my cheek. We watch *Million Dollar Listing Los Angeles*, our guilty pleasure, and imagine that we live in a modern turnkey on the sea in Malibu where the bedroom is comprised fully of windows looking right out on the waves.

"Babe, if only there were a dry beach," he says.

"We can live with a wet/dry for now. We'll just suntan when the tide is down," I reply.

When the pain hits me hard, he has a bowl of weed packed and ready, and steady doses of painkillers that he makes me take with lightly buttered cinnamon toast so that I won't throw up. He rubs my shoulders as I rock back and forth on my knees on the living room floor and he says that he's sorry.

"It feels like it's so deep inside," I tell him. I know that he can't understand this pain and I want him to. "It's constant like a stomach-ache and it's radiating like a broken ankle and it's burning like a hot stone pushed into the skin. It's everything, all at once."

He draws me a hot bath and though I'm hesitant, I try it. Once I submerge, my body stops convulsing, everything relaxes.

"This really feels amazing," I tell him with tears in my eyes. "You know, my grandmother tried to abort my mother by taking a hot bath."

I lay my head back onto the hard edge of the tub.

"Is that a thing?"

"Well, back then, it was like something women said could work but that probably rarely, if ever, did. Anyway, it didn't work for her, obviously."

He leans back and pushes himself up to sit on the sink counter. "Why'd she try to do it?"

"She was so depressed, and her pregnancies always made it worse, she just didn't want to go through it again," I say.

"Babe," he says. He points at the tub with a horrified glare.

A bloody chunk shaped like a tiny tongue lingers between my legs. Around it swirls of blood spiral towards the surface of the water. It must look so grotesque to him, he's probably, or surely, imagining that it's our aborted child. For some reason I laugh.

"It's just my uterus lining and some blood," I say matter of factly. "It looks that way with my period too; it's fine." *Just cells. Five weeks and five days.*

After the bath, he walks me to the bed as I curve hunched over my aching stomach. He gets me a heating pad, another half of a painkiller, and a glass of whiskey with ice, which I'm still sipping as I drift off to sleep. He checks on the heating pad for me during the night to make sure that it's safe and not too hot, as it is old with a yellow and grey flowered print and a frayed wire. It belonged to my grandmother, now dead ten years, and I refuse to get a new one so long as it still works. I imagine she must have clutched it to her own stomach many a time, wishing away the pains of her life.

✦ ✦ ✦

When I tell my best friend Betty about the abortion over the phone the following morning, she says, "What has become of us when we care more about scuba diving trips than the prospect of bringing a life into the world?"

This is not offensive because the "we" refers to her and me. We are in this thing together now. We are the kind of women who are in their thirties but aren't married with 2.5 children, don't have a house and at least two types of acceptable pets. She calls us "outside cats," and she no longer believes that we'll ever be able to properly fit into the societal norms. She thinks we've gone too far, seen too much, thought too hard, lost any affinity we may have had towards "normalcy." I'm not totally sure that I agree with her. Nor do I disagree.

"But I'll be fine, right?" I ask her. "I mean if I go for the dive even though I shouldn't. I'm not like risking my safety in a real way, am I?" I'm looking for her vote of confidence, which is usually easily won.

"It's basically a bad period from this point out," Betty assures me. "You passed the hard part. Everyone's just covering their asses."

I'm walking down Montana Avenue towards the ocean. The street is speckled with well-off white women toting small dogs, expensive clothing stores, coffee shops, and perfectly interspersed trees. I hope that no one passing knows what I am discussing, what I have done.

"You know what cracks me up?" she asks.

"What?"

"The whole dichotomy of the thing. Like if you're going to keep the baby, you immediately stop doing anything dangerous or putting anything bad into your body. You run to the nearest health food store to purchase high quality prenatal vitamins, you throw out all the coffee, alcohol, and high fructose corn syrup, and you immediately do as many sets of bun burners and crunches as humanly possible, knowing that your body isn't going to look like it does now EVER again. Whereas, if you're not going to keep the baby..." She takes a well-timed pause.

"Upon seeing the two blue lines," she continues, "you immediately have a drink, smoke a bowl, drive to the clinic where you stick a bunch of terrible chemicals in your body to turn against what your body is trying to do for you. All the while, your poor, confused uterus, which has finally been activated on the most complex and insane task ever imaginable—growing a human life—is suddenly shocked to a halt. The proverbial alarms sound. The green light turns unexpectedly red."

"A false start," I say.

"Exactly!" she replies.

"Maybe you should make that some kind of stand-up act," I suggest to her. She chuckles, one time, hard.

I flash a brief smile into my phone but quickly grow sad in thinking about the fact that she's had two abortions and that I know nothing about them, really, except that they were had. We never discussed what her experiences were like, how she felt during or after or since. No details, lessons, or emotions. What kind of friends did that make us? Was this lack of sharing due to her shame or was it my failing as a friend not to have asked more pointed questions? I suddenly want to tell her, to tell every person that I consider a friend, every detail of what my abortion was like, every single strange sensation that is flooding through me. I want to tell them so that they will never have to feel like it's something that can't be discussed or shared. I open my mouth to begin some sort of confession, but Betty cuts in before I have the chance to get anything out...

"To be honest," she says, and I think for a moment that she's going to offer me up something profound, something real and true, something to make it all make sense, "I'm more worried about the sharks than anything else. Is it true that menstrual bleeding attracts sharks? You be careful down there. Please don't get eaten, I couldn't bear it."

"I won't get eaten," I assure her. We exchange quick good-byes and my chapped lips seal closed in the California sunshine.

◆ ◆ ◆

Anacapa Island pops volcanic brown against the crisp blue of the sky and the Pacific Ocean that surrounds it. The expansive island rock comes out of nowhere in the middle of the ocean and even when you are right up upon it, it hardly seems real. It is the second smallest of the Channel Islands in Ventura County, at about 5 miles long. Fittingly, Anacapa means mirage.

Our dive boat, The Explorer, rocks back and forth as we make our way. Troy holds my waist as we rise and fall together at the ocean's will. The day is so clear it is unnerving. I feel like I'm on the set of a movie with a perfectly fake island backdrop behind me. Troy is the love interest lead, the good-looking man who will neither break up with nor settle down with the devoted protagonist. *What silly dramas we play out in this life.*

The ride out to the Channel Islands is long, about two hours, and requires a bit of Dramamine even for those not normally cursed with seasickness. On my first trip out when I didn't take any, the sensation was almost exactly like the one bout of morning sickness I woke up with, which had alerted me to 'the pregnancy' in the first place. It's been three days, and all of my pain from the abortion has ceased. I have taken my Dramamine, and I really feel fine. The whole ordeal behind me. The only thing I have left to worry about is putting on my impossibly thick 7mm wetsuit, and gearing up with weights, tank, BCD, hoses, gloves, boots, fins, mask. Oh, and the tampon that I'm not supposed to be wearing to withhold my still heavy bleeding, and the lingering anxiety about entering the ocean with my cervix still open.

When all my gear is on and tested, I hold my face mask with one hand and my regulator with the other, jumping fins first off the boat. Once the water absorbs the weight of all the gear—and I pass the initial anxiety of descending—my mask tightens to my face, my ears equalize, and my body relaxes towards the bottom of this place.

Everything becomes vivid and present, the way all life should be.

I touch the sandy bottom of the ocean and look around to orient myself. The spiky metal anchor of The Explorer hooks the ocean floor behind me and ahead I can see nothing but kelp forests, rock crests, and clear water flecked with fish. I hold my hands still and maintain my buoyancy. The fish don't seem to mind me. A deep orange Garibaldi swims up, its black beady eyes meeting mine. Troy floats nearby; he's a bright blue and yellow creature inhabiting this strange world as easefully as he inhabits the one above. I give him the okay sign to let him know I'm doing well, and he pulls out his air for a moment to blow me a dramatic kiss. This is my first real dive, unaccompanied by an instructor, since my recent certification course. It feels like freedom to wander this world.

The water takes hold of me. The breeze turns to tide and the kelp trains sway gently from side to side along with me, everything under the water dancing silently together. There are innumerable florescent coral puffs in purple and pink, secret rock worlds. There's a lobster hiding in the shadows, upright and alert like an old man in the doorway, like my own father so often on the lookout for visitors or intruders on the dead-end New Jersey street I grew up on. I wonder what my father would think of my abortion. He never judged me harshly, almost incapable of seeing my flaws, but I think it would have made him sad that there could have been a new little life born from me for him to love. Perhaps if he were still alive and could meet my child, I would feel differently about everything.

I listen to the sound of my oh-so-human inhales and exhales, oozing loudly in and out of the second stage of my regulator like the deepest yoga breath. I enjoy the feeling of the water surrounding me and nothing more. No industry, no factory smoke stacks, housing developments, storefronts advertising exquisite this or that. There are no people walking briskly with judging downturned eyes. The noises of life, of motorcycles, music, voices, sirens, have been muted.

I feel suddenly "wombed"—the complete submergence, breathing underwater through a cord. I have been here before. It seems suddenly so natural that I was once an unformed being inside a watery organ, a place I grew too large for and exploded forth from, in the same way that I will someday have outlived my stay on earth and vanish to another unknown. The whole cycle of life seems to make sense. I wish that I could show this world to the nice pink-scrubbed nurse. I wish that I could tell her that I hope someday to feel the call of motherhood the way I feel the call, now, towards the bottom of the sea.

I take a deep inhalation of my dry oxygen and exhale bubbles that grow and float above me like a cluster of translucent jellyfish glistening in the sun streams that slice the water above in majestic lines. I want to cry but I'm afraid of what that might be like with a face mask and regulator. I want to cry because I feel closer than I ever have before to a thing not called 'the pregnancy.' Closer, not to a grouping of coincidental cells, but to something else. A choice. A someday soul submerged deep inside myself, a great and beautiful possibility that at forty feet under, I can almost align with, I can almost believe in and understand.

✧ ✧ ✧

Catie Jarvis is an author of fiction, as well as a yoga instructor, a competitive gymnastics coach, and an English and writing professor. She received her B.A. in writing from Ithaca College, and her M.F.A. in creative writing from the California College of the Arts. She grew up on a lake in northern New Jersey and now lives by the ocean in California with her husband, her baby daughter Skywalker and lots of surfboards. She finds the world to be a strange place and loves writing that examines the ambiguity of "reality." Her debut novel, "The Peacock Room," is available on Amazon. Find more about the author and her writing at CatieJarvis.com and 30inLA.com. Follow her on IG @30inLA.

4

The Keeper

I was seven years old when I started collecting secrets. It wasn't on purpose; I didn't know what I was doing. All I knew was when Evan leaned in and said, "I like you very much, Emmie, and you can't tell a single soul," the words tumbled out of his mouth with a pinkish glow around them. He didn't seem to notice, as it was at that very moment he smacked his chapped lips against my lower cheek. His breath smelled like peanut butter, and when he pulled away, his face grew bright red like the summer sky at sunset. Giggling, he leaped out of the tree house, the boards creaking with the shift of weight. Evan disappeared into his home without a single look back.

The peach-colored words hung there for a moment, right in front of me, before they began to float upward like balloons that had just been set free. My hands reached before my brain could stop them. The words squirmed around inside my palms like lightning bugs, and I stuffed them into the pocket of my jean shorts.

Carefully, I climbed down the ladder. When I landed on the freshly cut grass, I was surprised to see Evan had returned. Instinctively, I kept my hand atop my pocket, afraid he'd notice the fabric moving and take his words back.

"My mom says she'll take us to Dairy Queen," Evan grinned, showcasing his missing front teeth.

We were next door neighbors and the same age, which is all one needs at seven years old to be best friends. We were together so often that we failed to be seen as separate people. We moved as one, talked as one, played as one. *"EmmieandEvan* spend far too much time in that tree house." *"EmmieandEvan* want to go to the movies." *"Emmieand-Evan* are missing again, has anyone seen them?"

But on that day, I felt separate. I was just Emmie.

I looked down at my light up sneakers and shuffled my feet. "But what about what you just said?" I mumbled.

"Oh, that?" Evan waved his hand and giggled all over again. "It was a secret. Just for you." He swung his arms back and forth. "I feel better saying it out loud."

But I didn't. My stomach felt flipped upside down, or maybe turned inside out. The words were still jumbled up in my pocket. I pressed down harder on the fabric.

"I have to go home."

Evan's smile disappeared. "No ice cream?"

"Not today," I said, running into my house. Through the living room, past my mother (*"No running inside, Emmie!"*), up the rickety staircase, into my bedroom, before I thrust myself into the back of my closet. All the while, the words swirled and swam.

I kept my allowance change in a mason jar hidden far in the back. After hunting around in the dark for it, my hands found the smooth glass surface. I pulled it out and dumped the change onto the hard-wood floor. The coins clinked and clattered as they spilled throughout the room, and I poured in the words to fill the jar's empty space.

◆ ◆ ◆

I soon learned there were two kinds of secrets.

Some secrets fit just fine in the jar in my closet, tucked behind my baby albums and forgotten Halloween costumes. Ones like when Evan told me he was really the one who broke his father's camera and blamed it on his sister, or my brother's whispered confession that he stole mom's cigarettes. Harmless. Silly. These secrets were bright oranges and teals and Kelly green. They intermixed together in the back of my closet, casting a warm glow into my room that only I could see.

The other secrets needed to be handled with more care. Hidden immediately, where no one else could find them. This happened to be my bookbag.

That was an accident. It was just because I was wearing it home on the last day of third grade when the first secret of this kind was revealed. Evan had been quiet, which wasn't like him at all. So, I asked. I wish I never did.

The dark red words shot out of Evan's mouth the second the tears rolled down his freckled cheeks. I didn't want to keep the words, looking as if they were blood-soaked, but taking the secrets always made the other person feel better. So, I reached out with a grimace and shoved them to the bottom of my backpack. My fingertips burned slightly, and my mouth asked, "where, " but my eyes begged, "don't tell." Evan rolled up his sleeve to reveal a large blue-and-purple bruise that wrapped all the way around his arm. He laughed, a breathy laugh that sounded more like a sob. When I didn't laugh with him, he quieted.

We turned the corner onto our street and there was a large truck outside Evan's home. Big, muscular men walked in and out with boxes. Evan sniffed.

"We are leaving," he said, before I could even process enough to ask the question.

"We?"

"My mom, sister, and me. We can't live with him anymore."

I nodded as if I understood. But really, I couldn't imagine Evan's world. Just as I couldn't imagine a world without Evan. He moved a few towns over and that was the end of *EmmieandEvan*. But his secret stayed with me, in the bottom of my bookbag.

◆ ◆ ◆

As I maneuvered my way through middle and high school, a few other secrets joined Evan's. A collection was formed. One I never wanted.

The maroon words that spilled from my brother as he told me he was taking these little round pills and I had better not tell Mom and Dad.

Into the bookbag.

The stormy gray words that encompassed me when a classmate whispered with nervous giggles that she was hooking up with our biology teacher in exchange for a higher grade.

Into the bookbag.

Or the Tuesday night I stayed up late working on an AP history project, and my mother stumbled in. She said she was returning from a work meeting, but the hickey on her neck said differently. I confronted her about it. Miraculously, she admitted it, stroking my hair and saying, "Emmie, I'm so sorry," over and over again. I led her to the couch, where she passed out as soon as her head hit the pillow. Her secret loomed in the kitchen, and if it had eyes, they would've burned a hole into me. I clenched my jaw and thought of alternatives. Finally, I stuffed it into my bookbag to get rid of the sight.

Those words were blacker than midnight.

By the end of high school, a few things had fallen apart: my parents' marriage, my brother's future, and my nine-year-old bookbag. I carried it everywhere, not even taking it off once I reached my seat in class. My textbooks hugged to my chest, my bookbag resting on my back. This was the way I navigated school. Navigated life.

Classmates teased me, asking why I didn't just use my bookbag. How was I supposed to tell them I didn't want my calculus textbook rubbing against my mother's affair? Shakespeare and Dickens intermixed with my brother's addiction?

My father bought me a brand new bookbag for college. Sturdy and vibrant and untarnished. Some name brand he must've been swindled into buying at the mall. When he gifted it to me, I didn't say a word. I slung my old bookbag to the front to rest on my torso, wrapping my arms tightly around the sack. My father sighed. It was no use.

I was chosen as the Secret Keeper, and I could never give up my bag filled with the most important ones. If I wasn't there to protect them, where would they go?

◆ ◆ ◆

I saw her the first Friday night of college. When my older cousin warned me I'd fall in love at least twelve times my freshman year, I had rolled my eyes and laughed. But then I saw her—the heart-shaped birthmark on her collarbone, the gentle curl of her strawberry blonde hair, the natural curve of her lips coated with peach-colored lipstick. I saw her, and it wasn't so funny anymore.

She was the one to open the apartment door for me, joking that this wasn't even her place and yet here she was.

Here she was.

My mouth became dry and I smacked my lips together, trying to find some words to say, any word. Literally any word at all. Her face broke into a wide smile, her green eyes sparkling.

"Oh, are you thirsty?" She handed me a red Solo cup of jungle juice, before being swept away by the crowd. I watched as she floated around the apartment, socializing in an effortless way that I both envied and admired. When she glanced my way, she pushed her hair back from her face and locked eyes with me. My heart just about jumped into my throat.

"Yo, who wears a bookbag to a party," a voice sniggered from behind me. A chorus of laughter broke out, and my face burned. I didn't have the courage to see who said it. I didn't have the courage to see if the girl had heard it. I downed my jungle juice, tightened my bookbag straps, and promptly turned to leave.

I would've been successful, and had a perfectly quiet night in my dorm, if my bookbag hadn't gotten caught on the door handle and let out a large rip. It sounded like a stack of papers being torn in half.

The roaring laughter surrounded me from all sides. I frantically tried to walk forward, squirming and twisting, but could still feel my backpack firmly stuck on the handle. The rip deepened, and I gasped as if it were me.

"What's wrong with all of you?" came an angry voice. I turned to see the back of the girl. She stood with her hands on her hips, shielding me from the crowd. Of course, it had to be her. "Can't you see she needs help?"

The laughter dissolved into murmurs and weak apologies. I looked down, sure my face was a blazing red. My whole body was warm now. I tried once more to leave, and heard a soft, "Just wait."

Very gently, she unhooked my bag from the handle. She was so close I could smell her scent of French vanilla and lavender, even above the strong party fumes of cheap alcohol and sweat.

"Be careful," she said. Her voice was just as soft as the touch of her fingers on my forearm.

35

We stepped out of the apartment and into the quiet hallway. She tucked a strand of hair behind her ear, eyeing my bag. "It looks like you have a tear on the bottom."

I swung the bookbag around to assess the damage. The tear was much bigger than I expected, and the colors of the secrets shimmered. I clutched the bag tightly to my chest, careful not to let any secrets escape.

"Thank you," I managed to mumble as I turned to leave.

"Hey," she said. "Let me help."

I shook my head quickly. "That's alright. It's super old anyway."

"No, *let me help*," she said sternly, touching my shoulder now. "That's a lot for one person."

We stared at each other and time slowed down. She took me by the hand, hers soft and delicate and perfect, and I followed.

I learned her name was Sophie. She was a year older than me, a sophomore, and studying psychology. She had big plans for the future; she was going to help so many people. She didn't laugh when I told her I was an undecided major. Didn't laugh when I told her I was undecided about everything in life.

The two of us walked around the campus, eerily quiet on such a warm August night. What a sight to see, I thought. Me, hugging my ratty bag. Her, walking with such purpose. It took everything in me not to stare.

As we arrived at a field just off campus, I wrapped my arms even tighter. I could feel the secrets bouncing around inside, a feeling so familiar. Words once spoken, whispered, shouted, whimpered. They all rumbled inside, sensing something was off.

Sophie took the bag away from me. She didn't ask, and I didn't fight her. I watched as she unzipped it. Reaching in, she grabbed the first secret. The crimson red words that Evan once muttered so many years ago. Suddenly I was in third grade again, feeling my hands shake as I watched the movers truck carry Evan away.

The red reflected in Sophie's eyes. "You can see them?" I asked.

She gazed at me softly. "Yes. I can see them."

She tossed the words from her hands, allowing them to disappear into the night sky and live amongst the stars. We were silent for a moment, before taking turns to reach in for the next. And the next. Red, gray, maroon, black. We watched them go, floating upward and upward, and then they were gone.

✧ ✧ ✧

Paige Gardner is a lover of all things fiction. She enjoys writing novels, flash fiction, and short stories. Paige grew up in a small, unassuming town outside Pittsburgh, graduated from Penn State University, and moved to Bucks County, PA to pursue a career in the nonprofit field. She is the co-founder of Dandelion Revolution Press, and a member of the Bucks County Writers Group. When Paige isn't writing, she enjoys performing on stage, reading books of all genres, enjoying the company of close friends, and laughing. She doesn't know how this collection found its way to your hands, but she's glad it did. To keep up with Paige's writing journey, you can follow her on Twitter at @JPaige Gardner.

5

WHEN WATER SINGS

Kilkenny, Spring 1740

When my mother was pregnant with me, it rained for nine months without stopping. This was Ireland so no one thought it was that out of the ordinary. An extraordinary coincidence. A miracle. A curse.

The day I slipped out of my mother, "like a mermaid so blue ye were, with yere lips puckered like a fish," my granny has told me, was the day it stopped raining. But it didn't stop, not really. It just poured *in* me instead. My body hummed when water was near. I could feel it move.

When the pigs across the farm knocked over their trough as I lay in bed nearly asleep, I sloshed inside. When a great bubbly gray cloud painted the sky, my muscles tensed. When I lay in the eastern field hiding from my chores, I could sense rather than hear when Granny lowered the pail into the well.

An entire pregnancy with nothing but rain affected my mother. Most dreadfully. I was three when she filled her dress pockets with stones and walked into the River Nore.

After that, water filled my father's eyes any time he looked at me. Even if it didn't spill, I felt it swollen there.

"Yere the spitting image of yere mother, ye are *a stóirín*." He'd pat my little head of red, fluffy curls and repeat over and over, "*a stór, a stóirín*." *My treasure, my little treasure.*

But I was not worth enough to get him to stay. The Town said he was too young a lad to raise a daughter. Rumors flew as they always did in our small town. Kilkenny was like a cross woman with round hips, but a kind heart when it suited. And I think my father left to get away from that too.

I lived with my grandparents after that.

Father rewed a lass a couple of towns over and took over her family's farm. They had a brood of boys. I was glad of this. Anytime I took the poor dapple mare to visit, I followed the river that my mother drowned herself in. I pretended my mother was a river goddess and had become her true self when she waded into the water and never came out. I'd talk to her, telling her, "I'm going to see father and the lads. I wonder if they've gotten any new animals."

She'd reply, *whoosh, perhaps they have, Niamh, whoosh, whoosh.*

When I arrived at their farm, they'd take my hand and drag me around, forcing me to find all the wet patches in the fields and near the barns and out in the woods. I'd close my eyes and close my ears, concentrating on hearing the water *inside*. When I could feel it murmur soft poetic things, I knew it talked to the other water nearby. I followed the threads of their conversations. The heavy glug or the gentle swish of wind moving the surface of a stagnant pool. My brothers and I skipped, giggling as our feet stomped in miniature seas and created tides on land.

If my emotions were high (as they sometimes were when I talked to the River Nore and heard no reply), I could make a little puddle swirl or a pond have a current. We'd drop dried leaves and see whose went to the other side first. The lads often turned over rocks and poked things with sticks, stirring sleeping newts to show their speckled, smooth coats of brown and yellow.

Splashing turned to spitting turned to me wishing I had a sister.

My childhood with Granny and Grandpa was decidedly slower. More like a trickling brook and less like the river that secretly raged inside of me. But I didn't mind. They were kind, hardworking, pious people. Grandpa snuck me extra slices of tart and told Granny, "that ol' mouse was back in the cupboard again." Granny hummed hymns as she churned butter or spun yarn or baked bread. They let me roam and dream and find water all over the farm.

One would think I was a melancholy child and yet I thrived. My blood constantly sang. To have singing blood was to have a singing soul.

I had no trouble ever discovering water. It was quite useless to have a gift to detect water when one lives on such a wet and rainy island.

Then came the Drought.

◆ ◆ ◆

The winter before the Drought was the Great Frost. Almost everyone's potato crops that were not buried below the frost line and froze became inedible and unplantable for next season.

I moved our crop on account of my gift. I felt the frost dipping lower, lower, lower. Penetrating all the layers of dirt even in storage gardens and fields. I felt the little ice shards spearing the precious spuds. In a deep turfy moulded garden, we stored all the potatoes and they were saved. At first, the Town called us lucky.

That spring, the rains never came.

Everything was used to being waterlogged. And suddenly, everything and everyone was less bogged down by the constant cloak soaking mist. At first, people celebrated.

"An entire week of sunshine. Can ye believe our luck? The good Lord has blessed us this spring," Granny crooned, shaking out her stiff limbs.

By the end of the second week, people started to get wary. They still felt grateful and thanked the good Lord after every meal and twice on Sunday. Everyone tilled and seeded their fields in the sun.

Even though the sun shined, the air never warmed. It remained cold and the wind fierce. It was like the winter kept going but summer was teasing us. There was no spring to be found in their feud and we suffered.

Granny sat in our little farmhouse darning a pair of stockings, her brows furrowed so that it covered her stone blue eyes. The thin skin under her eyes shone the watery green veins beneath. If my blood thrummed with water, hers thrummed with land; while I could feel the water move, she knew by instinct alone what the plants needed without even asking them.

When we entered the third week without rain, our black cattle started waning. The once rolling hills never turned their lush, vivid green after the winter. They remained dull and brown. The scattering of stones was more visible without the stubborn lichen sticking to their surface. The trees seemed to lean and grow smaller. Birds spent more and more of their time near the ever dwindling River Nore. I couldn't hear my mother at all now.

Kilkenny had taken care of me my whole life. She was our feisty mother hen who kept her brood under her wing. The Town became cranky and lashed out at her children. A barn burned down. A baby was born without breath. The Town's milky face was now red and chapped with the dust that blew on her streets.

"This is payment because it rained for nine months when yere mother—God rest her soul—was carrying ye. Now it'll be dry for nine months, mark my words. The Almighty knows this winter was the coldest and driest it's ever been. It's not right, Niamh. It's not right."

Granny's desperation became my desperation. I longed to be useful and to actually have a gift that mattered. My limbs itched with the dry parched land and my soul ached to be reunited with its secrets. The subdued pulsing in my veins and the almost silent singing of the heart within my heart. I could find the water we so desperately needed for irrigation.

So, I did.

Once again, the Town called us lucky.

◆ ◆ ◆

One cannot help but believe in God when one entered the Cathedral Church of Saint Canice. It dwarfed all other buildings and its spires and medieval tower could be seen for miles. It beckoned the faithless with its quiet foreboding power. It was our Town's warm cradling arms.

The Town was abuzz with gossip of a newcomer. The news took Kilkenny's mind off of her parched tongue and cracked lips. She smiled through the bloody lips and relished in the distraction. A young widow had come to live on her late husband's abandoned property on the outskirts.

A hymn rose up and lifted me with it. *And let there be water that were gathered and called the Sea.* It lingered in the wood lapped ceiling shaped like bog-rosemary.

I tied my bonnet tighter under my chin, containing my mass of auburn curls. It was a Sunday service in late April and Lent had almost passed. Times were so desperate, the church allowed us to eat meat four days a week, if we could obtain it. We had the river for some fish at least. But not many. The beggars had starved and passed. They were desperate from the winter, their skin jagged with bones. Now their bones were turning to dust.

Spring days in Kilkenny were often moody affairs that breathed down yere neck with thick, foggy air. Cold one minute, warm the next. But this day was the opposite of thick. The air was thin, cold; the whispers were thick, sticky.

I stared at the new lass through a sea of hats and bonnets, high collared coats and scarves. She turned her head to look at the alcove dedicated to St. Canine who expelled all the druids from Kilkenny. In her profile, I could see that she didn't have an eye, it was just sealed shut. She had a soft jaw and all I could see of the rest of her head was a couple of loose locks of black hair.

Mr. and Mrs. Walsh introduced themselves to her when the service ended. They looked more like siblings than husband and wife, both with curly hair the color of burnt bread.

"It is a pleasure to make yere acquaintance. I am Mrs. Meabh O'Manacháin." Her voice dropped lower. "My husband passed away this winter." She bowed her head, touched her gloved fingers to her forehead and her chest. Then she stopped, unable to finish the cross.

The thin air got thinner. It was like no one surrounding her could breathe and I watched them all suck on dry air.

"I am so sorry for yere loss, Widow O'Manacháin."

To be a widow so young and beautiful, I thought, *was almost a tragedy.* Almost.

"What brings ye to Kilkenny?" Mr. Walsh asked.

"My late husband—God rest his soul—had property a mile from here."

I snorted under my breath. A man would definitely gobble her up despite her one eye. Widow O'Manacháin swiveled towards me with a ghost of a smile on her lips like she knew what I was thinking. I gave her a small smile in return.

"Ye must mean the Golden Valley farm," Mrs. Walsh said.

"Yes, that's the one."

"Hmm, they say that farm is cursed," her husband added.

"Shhhh," the wife said, and swatted his arm.

I didn't hear the rest as Granny linked arms with me as we exited soberly down the center aisle and out the cathedral.

"Niamh, I *must* see ye settled before I am buried," Granny said. She must have overheard the young widow's story too. "Ye are already two and twenty. Yere mother made me promise to see ye properly wed."

I knew this was a lie. My mother was too down to talk much. But perhaps it's what she would have wanted. To see me with a husband and have children of my own. Even if the thought repulsed me.

I swallowed a sigh and looked down at my feet. Out of the left corner of my eye I could spot rounded gravestones, discoloration stains streaked their faces with charcoal tears.

"Ye must pay a visit to that new widow."

I raised my head. "Yes," I agreed, too quickly.

◆ ◆ ◆

"Good morning," I called tentatively, walking through the tall grass towards Widow O'Manacháin's farmhouse. House was a generous term for the dilapidated cottage and half eaten barn nestled into the overgrown goldenrod.

"Hallo!" she replied, opening the door. A smile pulled easily across her face. "Come in."

I did so and was engulfed by a toasty room that smelled of strong lye soap. A stone mortar with grain sat on a kitchen table ready to be turned into flour.

"I brought ye some preserves," I told her, raising a jar of pickled cabbage.

"That is most kind." She took the jar and stored it in a cupboard. Without her bonnet obscuring her face, she was stunning. Her face was heart-shaped and smooth. A round blue-black eye and, where the other should have been, a smooth patch of skin. A long thick plait hung down the length of her back. She had softly sloped shoulders and a rounded backside. She took an apron off a hook next to the cupboard and tied it right at the bottom curve of her spine. My eyes lingered.

I cleared my throat. "Can I help ye with anything, Widow O'Manacháin?"

"Oh, please call me Meabh." She pinched the hem of her apron in her fingers, her knuckles white. "Now tell me, is this farm really cursed?" She raised an eyebrow.

I laughed and told her it wasn't.

"That's too bad," she said. "I thought it could keep men away."

I couldn't help but smile. "Well, I can spread a mean rumor that it is?"

"Would ye? Might get ye in trouble."

"I'd welcome a bit of trouble. This town is dull... at times, anyway. That or much too interested in yere personal affairs. Or lack thereof," I muttered.

Her one eye squinted as she sat down at her kitchen table, gesturing for me to join her. I did so.

"What's yere name, lass?"

"Niamh ó Séaghdha." Reaching across the table, I worked the grain with the stone pestle. "Like the daughter of the god of the sea."

She hummed. "Just like the goddess, beautiful ye are. Beautiful and bright."

My face went warm and I knew my neck and chest were splotchy with patches of red. My insides hummed, and I could feel water deep under the ground. Impossibly deep and hidden. But she made me feel it.

I wondered what happened that made her leave town.

"I came here to get away from trouble," she confided in me, as if she had read my private thoughts.

"Of yere late husband?"

"'Tis true that the memories of him linger all over Waterford, but the town's unkindness to me after he died is why," she shook her head. "We were only wed seven months, ye see. As they debated whether or not to allow me to live in his cobbler shop. I sold what I could and came here."

"What happened?" I asked, not sure why she was telling me this. Maybe because I was the only one in town near her age and not wed.

"He had a weak chest and the cold took him. No one believed someone so young would die so suddenly." She looked down at her hands and then shrugged.

✦ ✦ ✦

I went over the next day. And the following. For three weeks we found excuses to bring each other little gifts or help each other weed the garden or chase crows off the seeded fields.

We were as thick as thieves. My family blamed her for my lack of interest in suitors. But the truth was, marriage held little interest to me. The idea of being touched in that carnal way made me cringe and dry up. And I was someone whose body swam and sang. I longed for a companion to share my life with, but not more than that.

"Will ye come with me?" Meabh asked one evening.

I gave her a look that told her she didn't have to ask. She grabbed my hand with a huge, toothy grin on her face that made her one eye squint. It was almost sunset so we both donned coats and she grabbed a lantern with a lit candle inside.

She took me behind the barn where there was a great patch of trees. We cut through the underbrush to a well-worn path in the weeds and wildflowers. What would normally be bright green had turned a sickly yellow.

We arrived at a glade where a ceramic bowl and an unlit smudge sat in the middle. Great boulders were placed at the markings of the compass and, judging by the thick covering of moss, they had been there for a long time.

My friend knelt in the grass in front of the ceramic bowl and placed the lantern beside her with a clink. She opened the door and lit the smudge. Blowing on the embers, she waved it around herself first from head to toe; incense of sage and lavender and heather filled the glade.

I stood on the edge and watched her get up. She danced around the stone on the southern point of the circle, a trail of sweet smelling smoke behind her. Her arms were lifted high above her as her relaxed head slowly followed. Spinning and spinning in a haze of smoke and dull light, she swayed like grass in the wind. The twilight hour streaked through the tree leaves in ribbons of purple.

She went back to the ceramic bowl and placed the smudge inside before taking a white veil from her pocket and placing it over her head and face. She bowed down to the north, the east, the south, the west. She stood facing south, and I was right out of the corner of her good eye. She either winked or blinked at me. She rose both of her arms in a great wave, and a strong warm southern breeze barreled past us and made the tips of our uncovered hair lift and dance.

I stepped fully into the glade and took her hands in mine. She did not flinch. She did not smile. But her shoulders were relaxed and her flushed cheeks soft.

I didn't think of my gift as witchcraft. It was just water after all. I couldn't summon the devil or possess vulnerable children. I was just in tune with the elements like the druids of old. As a child, I heard stories about faeries taking babies and replacing them with sickly faerie ones. Seal women luring men into the water to drown. But me? I wasn't magical.

I shook my head. This was not a gift from the faeries but a gift from my mother. The only part of her I had left. I had never heard of someone like me, born with the ability to hear water sing.

I told her this. I told her my secret. Her eye crinkled softly and she grabbed my hand.

She told me she learned this from her mother too, who was a sort of healer. We laughed and cried and went back to her farmhouse with elbows linked. I could hear water singing beneath my feet and a warm —not cold—breeze tickle my neck.

Before I went inside, I looked over my shoulder and saw a man shrouded in the twilight hour standing on the road with a basket. A suitor, to try and woo the young widow. He pulled his hat low, turned around, and left.

✦ ✦ ✦

A week later, the Town had started to talk. At church on Sunday, I overheard Mr. and Mrs. Walsh as they whispered conspiratorially to each other. Their eyes darting from me to Meabh, their curly hair of burnt bread swaying as they talked.

"What luck those two young lasses have," Mrs. Walsh said.

"Luck?" Mr. Walsh scoffed. "Water *and* warm air for their crops alone? That's more than luck."

A shiver unfurled down my spine like a roll of parchment. Not at all smooth or quick. Their suspicions would turn to gossip by the afternoon, and I knew I had to keep my head down and not see Meabh. She might not have been my sister by blood, but she was my sister now.

As I walked home with my grandparents, Granny said, "That way you have water, I never thought of it as anything more than coincidence. But, Niamh, it will be a curse on our farm."

My blood went ice cold and I clenched my fists. To hear my own granny believe the suspicions meant I could do naught but pretend we struggled like the rest. Determined to keep my distance, I rushed over to Golden Valley Farm to tell Meabh what I heard...and say good-bye for now.

"We must be careful," I urged.

Meabh didn't answer but continued to sweep the floor and direct the dust and particles into the smouldering hearth.

"Meabh..."

She stopped and leaned against the handle of the broom. "People always talk. I don't talk about my husband often—" she dug the toe of her shoe into the packed dirt, "—but we grew up together, ye know. No one could believe that he wanted to wed a lass with one eye."

An eye she was simply born without. I took the broom from her and directed her to sit down.

"He was a kind, good man! Poor of health. He always was really. I am not a blooming flower myself, so everyone thought we made a good enough pair. But after the Great Frost took him... The people of Waterford thought maybe I had killed him."

I paused at her bedside table. "Why? Yere a gentle soul. How could they believe such a thing?"

"We were wed less than a year and I would have all his money. I left to get away from the cruel rumors and start anew."

I wanted to tell her how glad I was that she came here. But it seemed unfair that her tragedy brought her to me. I reached aimlessly for her Bible on the table to straighten it.

When I grasped the spine, something bit my finger. A sharp pain pinching my calloused skin. I screamed, flinging the Bible across the room.

"What?" Meabh said, standing up, her chair falling over with a crash.

"A rat!" I exclaimed as it scurried away under the bed.

Meabh came over and took the broom to chase after the vermin, ready to crush it to death. "Nasty things," she huffed. "There's a hole somewhere and they keep getting in."

We heard a gasp and spun around to the doorway. Miss Doyle stood there, her hands over her mouth. The Town was always there, always watching. She ran.

For the second time that day, my body went cold, frosting over and icicles piercing my gut, my back, my neck. I walked over and picked up the far flung Bible, its pages faced down on the floor. Stroking the pages flat, I picked at the chewed spine.

A drop of blood welled up on the tip of my finger and I wrapped it in the handkerchief that was tucked up my sleeve.

We hadn't even got the fire going for our midday meal when a group of hulking men from the Town burst into the small one roomed home.

"Get them," neighbor MacLiam motioned to his other henchmen.

"What? No! What is happening?" I fumbled both with words and limbs, my feet tripping over each other as I backed up.

"Witches, both," Miss Doyle hissed.

Meabh screamed and collapsed. I scratched at the men as they grabbed me, grunting and grinding my teeth.

"No!" I screamed over and over, my voice going hoarse as the words grated past my clogged windpipe. As the lump formed in my throat and my limbs shook. My eyes were clear like crystal as my blood rushed. *Whoosh, whoosh, whoosh.*

As I twisted in their bruising grip, they heaved me outside and down the road. My toes dragged through the thick grass.

"Granny!" I called. "Help me!" I looked over my shoulder where men heaved Meabh like a sack of grain. "Meabh? Meabh! Help us!" Continuing to struggle only tightened the men's hold on me and I winced.

As we were dragged into town, people stood in their doorways and watched the proceedings like it was a parade. Kilkenny leaned into her hips and pursed her lips. It was like she had shut the door in my face. After I had been kind to her and neighborly, I realized I was nothing. I was not worth an ounce of her care. My heart wretched and split it two.

The commotion summoned everyone to watch our shame as the sheriff stood next to the open grate of the thieves' hole. Un-ceremoniously, Meabh and I were pushed to the opening. It was no use fighting or fleeing. The bloated crowd blocked any route of escape. I climbed down the ladder into the damp, empty hole. Dirt sprayed down, showering my hair as I bumped against the confined walls. I fell the last couple of feet, splayed on the rough ground of stone and slime. I groped on the floor as Meabh started to climb down and blocked all the light.

A rat crawled over my feet and I swished my skirts. I held a hand to my friend and helped her to the ground. The metal grate slid into place with a screech, thump. A couple of people clapped.

"This is wrong!" I shouted. I clung to the ladder and declared, "We are not witches!"

"Help us, please," Meabh begged more softly.

We pleaded to an unsympathetic crowd until we could see no more feet standing around the grate.

Despite it being a thieves' hole, it held more than thieves: adulterers, vagrants, murderers... suspected witches. Sinners all.

As the sun went down, a passerby flung a stale piece of bread and an old potato. My stomach was rolling, but I forced myself to take a bite of each before insisting that Meabh eat the rest. My dry tongue felt like a heavy hide, bristly and stiff.

When the sun drew up a black blanket over itself, the darkness was so complete I could not see my hand in front of my face. I wished for a blanket now. Meabh and I huddled together for warmth, holding onto one another for dear life. We didn't speak. There wasn't much to say.

So much for being as thick as thieves.

✦ ✦ ✦

When they dragged us out of the thieves' hole early the next morning, my eyes blinked rapidly to adjust to the harsh difference in light. My head was splitting with pain, having slept upright against Meabh's shoulder.

They didn't leave us in there for long. One could say we were lucky to have our own examiners in Kilkenny. As we were tugged through the center courtyard in town, boys gathered dry brush and whacked each other with it. The men had already constructed a great platform where two stout poles stood erect. Logs and branches were piled beneath.

"We'll be fine, Niamh," Meabh lied, her throat was parched and strained. Mine was too dry to even reply. I simply nodded, trying to hide the tears that betrayed me.

The men delivered us to the church and an examiner opened the door. The inside had been transformed into a place for a performance, complete with a stage and pulpit for us. This would be the trial—the entertainment—of the decade.

People in town were angry, their ruddy faces redder, their fists clenched. And it was convenient to be mad at us. They were already gathered, waiting for the show. Something to ease the burden of the dry spring.

In the pew where my family usually stood for service, Granny clutched tight to Grandpa. My father was there, along with his boys and his wife blooming with child. I swallowed hard. My little brothers had wide, mournful eyes. To them, I was just playing games. Now they knew there was a price to secrets.

"This is a farce," Granny cried, detaching herself from my grandpa. She used her wide hips to carve a path through the crowd. "A sham! How dare ye accuse mine kin as a witch!"

"Take her out!" the examiner called, not even lifting his head from his parchment.

"I have the right to speak for my granddaughter," Granny seethed. "To denounce this!" Her arms flailed and she couldn't even look at me.

"Grain and corn have died and it's *their* fault!" the Town cried, her voice high-pitched.

"Aye!" the crowd roared. "They cursed our crops!"

The next cry sent shivers down my spine.

"Burn them!"

I choked as a sob caught in the back of my throat. My eyes were so wide, and time seemed to slow. I blinked. And blinked. Their accusations, their fervor, built upon each other. Was there a way to stop them?

"Please," I begged, "we are women of God."

The examiners were unwavering, unmoved by the swaying crowd. "Let us call the first witness."

My granny let out a blood curdling scream. And my guards directed her out, more gently then they had me for which I was grateful. To be grateful when I was staring certain death in the face made me feel stronger, not weaker.

A witness came up to the stand: Mr. O'Brien, the man shrouded in shadow with the basket the night Meabh and I exchanged our pasts. He wrung his hat in his hands. He told the examiners and the growing crowd, "I'd seen them come out of the trees. A true faerie door is there. Everyone knows that. And I saw," he swallowed, "the widow had a veil of white over her head, not black."

Voices called from the crowd, "*Caillech*." Veiled one. "*Cailleach*." Witch.

"And the young lass," he pointed to me, "her hair was loose with wee flowers in it."

"He was way up on the road!" I exclaimed. "He doesn't know what he saw."

"Are ye calling this good man a liar?"

"No, but it was dark."

The examiner humphed. "Thank ye, Mr. O'Brien, for yere brave testimony. Next witness."

Miss Doyle failed to hide a smirk as she stood before the examiners and the crowd. "I went over to Golden Valley Farm to ask after the widow. But when I arrived, Niamh threw a Bible clear across the room."

Those watching made a *tisk-tisk*.

"They were performing satanic rituals! She even had blood all over her hands."

Miss Doyle was always a jealous creature. She took her misfortune at being a bastard out on the rest of her peers. I don't think the crowd believed her, yet they booed at us anyway.

Neighbor MacLiam mounted the witness stand next and told the examiners about his dying crops. How my family's farm thrived even though our fields were next to each other's. He laid out a calm and convincing argument that the examiners respected.

"Next witness," the examiners said.

Another witness? How could they have gathered so much evidence against us so quickly?

As we waited, a mysterious man called from the crowd, "She doesn't even live with her father!"

My father raised his voice for me for the first time in my life. "A grieving father is not fit to raise a daughter on his own." He faced me. "I'm sorry, *a stór.*"

I nodded and they left, the crowd parting for them like the sea for Moses. Tears streamed down my cheeks as I said a silent goodbye to my family. Again I was grateful they didn't have to see me like this. My father did not need to see me like this. I looked like my poor, sad mother. And now I was about to join her.

I was a fly in a spider's web. The web was not a sticky trap that I flew into. No, I was a fly, and the spider built its web around me and tried to convince me that I had flown into it all along. But I knew better.

The final witness sealed our fate.

Priest ó Cléirigh lifted the hem of his cassock and slowly ascended to the witness stand. He made the sign of the cross with downcast eyes.

"May God have mercy on the mortal souls present in this church today," he began, making another sign of the cross to the crowd. "These two women are not worshippers of the Lord but of the Devil himself!"

People exclaimed. A woman fainted.

This was the very town where St. Canice eliminated all the druid worshippers. And now, his predecessor, the priest of the church named in his honor, moved to eliminate us. The druids couldn't even flee to a mound for safety before the army overcame them. Like them, we were cornered from the start.

When the crowd finally settled, the priest went on. "They do not lift their voices to sing with us. Niamh would disgrace the Word of God by throwing the Bible. And this widow, she does not properly mourn her husband not six months gone from this world."

"Is it yere opinion that these two women are witches?"

"It is not my opinion. It is a fact."

The crowd exploded. People I had known my whole life. Teachers and neighbors and shop keepers. They yelled, throwing their hats down from the balcony, sweat and excitement inflating the air. The Town crossed her arms, nodding her head in justice. All I could smell was my own fear: sickly sweet like syrup, salty like the sea, stale like bread. It left a bad taste on my tongue.

I clung to Meabh, hyperventilating. She was quiet and pale as death. The same gruff men roughly grabbed our shoulders and tore us apart. I reached for Meabh again, tears streaming down my face. Water flowed out of her one eye and I could feel it leaving a trail of residue like a slug.

They didn't even take us back to the thieves' hole. Our fate was decided by a crowd looking to blame their bad fortune—our collective bad fortune—on two young lasses: too pretty, too different, too independent.

The crowd lifted us, and we surged outside the church to the pyre waiting to be lit. Like the lack of water that so plagued us, we were a tidal wave of hope for the Town. Hope that our demise would be their rebirth. That Kilkenny could rise from our ashes.

We were lashed to the pole on the platform to the sound of cheers. I scanned the crowd, but my grandparents were nowhere to be seen. My father nor his family. Struggling against the rope was no use and I looked over at my friend.

Meabh. Gentle, funny Meabh. With only one eye and the beauty of a druid goddess. She didn't deserve this. This was all my fault.

Torches were thrust under the platform and the dry sticks and brush caught instantly. Smoke, acrid and thick, gushed through the slates of wood under my feet. Meabh and I coughed as soot coated our exposed skin. It singed my nose and coated the back of my throat with bitter burning acid.

As the fire started to lick my toes, I stretched my soul. Searching and searching, outwards and upwards and downwards. Desperate to feel water sing to me. *Please*, I begged. *Please.*

The scorching flames crawled higher. Meabh screamed then coughed. Pain lanced through my core; her pain pierced my body and soul and I was undone. My skirt caught and I let out a scream.

We were burning. We were dying.

My heart pounded vigorously in my chest and I closed my eyes, concentrating. Wee droplets of water could be felt in the air. My blood pulled towards it. My blood wanted to be lifted higher and evaporate to join its kin. Hunching my shoulders, I pulled the water towards me.

I felt it snaking through the air, gathering in a great mass. From the air itself, water made my body hum once more.

You are strong, my mother crooned. *Niamh, my daughter of the sea.*

Gasps from the crowd and sharp intakes of breath broke my concentration. I noticed that Meabh was no longer screaming and I opened my eyes. *Rain.* Rain poured from the heavens. Swollen and sweet. Fat, twinkling drops drenched the parched ground and the parched souls of the people of Kilkenny.

The Town held out her arms and let the water fall on her face. She drank in the cool and her love swept through the cobbled streets. An extraordinary coincidence.

"It's a miracle," the priest said, kneeling in the forming mud. This spread through the crowd. A miracle.

The deluge of rain made the fire hiss and spit with anger before it sizzled and stopped. The dry, barren land flooded with water. My body was alive for the first time in months, buzzing with the water coating my skin.

"It's a sign from the Lord above," someone said. "They aren't witches!"

But we were. I was a witch. A curse.

"Release them."

And someone did. I didn't see who and I didn't really care. I was alive. Alive. My magic saved us. My eyes didn't move from Meabh as my breathing returned to normal.

"I love ye," I told her. As much as I could love, she was *a rúnsearc,* my secret love.

She nodded, a ghost of a smile on her lips. We were both still in shock, soaked through with cool blessed rain. A warm breeze rose from the south and a mild spring was upon us.

✦ ✦ ✦

Hayley E. Frerichs writes fantasy and historical romance in Bucks County, Pennsylvania. After graduating from Penn State with degrees in English and education, she fled adulthood and taught in southern Spain for a year. She loves to travel but is also content to stay at home with her sewing machine, tea kettle, and books. She is a co-founder and editor of Dandelion Revolution Press; her short story was featured in their first anthology, *Not Quite as You Were Told.* You can visit her website HayleyEFrerichs.com where she blogs about sustainable living and her many creative hobbies.

6

CAKE*

June fifteenth is my least favorite day of the year. I suppose as a college student I should hate finals week or the first day of the semester, or as a girl I should hate the day of the Victoria's Secret Fashion Show. I do hate them, sure, but the day that marks the middle of June is worse. I know I'm supposed to look forward to the day; it's an excuse to spend time with family and eat a shit ton of strawberry cake and mint chocolate chip ice cream. But I don't like strawberry cake and mint chocolate chip ice cream. Nina did. It's all my fault.

My parent's house is too silent now. You can no longer hear the mix of music that used to flow through the halls—for my dad, Luis Miguel; for my mother, Mozart. Jesse would play Green Day or whatever pop-punk band he was into, while I strictly listened to any folk music I could get my hands on. Nina would almost always listen to show tunes. She wanted to be an actress when she grew up.

Now, as I enter the house three years after Nina died, I'm met with silence. The only sounds I can hear are my brother's video games, muted by his closed door, and the clanking of glass as my mom digs through the kitchen cabinets. I follow the sounds of glass-on-glass and find my mom pouring herself a cheap pinot at the kitchenette table, a yearbook lying beside her. It's one in the afternoon. My carry-on suitcase rolls behind me and I lean it against the large counter, clearing my throat.

"Oh, Lydia!" Mom exclaims, trying to hide the glass of wine behind her as she stands in front of the table. "I didn't hear you come in. How

*Content notes: eating disorder, abduction

was the drive?"

"Not bad." Too short. "Is that Barefoot? Come on, mama, I drank that as a freshman."

"Don't let your father hear that," she jokes, walking over to give me a tight hug.

"That would require him talking to me," I say. I shut my eyes tightly as I squeeze her back, pulling away shortly after. "He still blames me, doesn't he?"

She gives me a sad smile and rubs my shoulder comfortingly. She doesn't say anything, though. She doesn't have to.

"How's therapy been?" she asks to change the subject.

I somehow keep myself from rolling my eyes. "Fine, Mom."

"And you're following the nutrition plan Dr. Goodrich gave you?"

"Jesus, Mom, yes," I say, not being able to control my eyes this time.

I can see that she wants to scold me for taking the Lord's name in vain, but she knows I would just point out she hasn't even been to church in three years. She nods her head instead, muttering a "good" before grabbing her wine and turning to leave the room.

The yearbook she was looking at before I came in still sits open on the table. I don't even have to look to know what page she was looking at—the memorial page dedicated to Nina. I've never seen it, never even opened my senior yearbook. I quickly snap the book shut, pushing it off the table and onto the nearest chair.

I turn on my heels quickly, grabbing my suitcase and dragging it down the hallway to the bedroom that used to be mine. I don't consider it my room, not anymore. It doesn't feel right considering I only sleep in it a few nights out of the year. I'm lifting my carry-on sized suitcase onto the bed when I hear a door creak open. Looking up, I see Jesse standing in the doorway, eyes red and dazed.

"Are you ready for this year's festivities?" I joke.

"Oh, totally. I can't wait to watch Dad complain about being lactose intolerant *after* he's had three bowls of ice cream," he answers, a lazy smirk crossing his face. Maybe it's fucked up to make jokes on my dead sister's birthday, but it's the only way to get through the fact that our parents still make us celebrate it.

I unpack the change of clothes and toiletries I brought as Jesse catches me up with all the neighborhood drama. The Simpsons' old dog died since I've been here last, but it's okay because their new dog doesn't climb under the fence and dig up our dad's flowers like the old one did. Judy Marshall told everyone at the last block party she voted for Trump. Cody Weston, a kid younger than me who was in the marching band in high school, got a DUI.

He seems to talk about everything besides the fact that his gap year between high school and college is coming to an end or how he got fired from Foot Locker.

◆ ◆ ◆

A couple of hours later, my mother declares that it's dinner time. Jesse and I quickly put eye drops in, reassuring each other that our eyes aren't red. I'm sure he's lying to me, but his eyes genuinely aren't. It's almost as if he's immune to it by now.

My mother unpacks the to-go food from Olive Garden as the rest of us meander into the dining room. She's heating it up and plating as if she cooked it herself—as if our kitchen has been used since Christmas. It's all my fault.

Jesse and I quickly put eye drops in, reassuring each other our eyes aren't red. I'm sure he's lying to me, but his eyes genuinely aren't. It's almost as if he's immune to it by now.

My father walks out of his office for the first time all night, and I can tell by the bags under his eyes and his wrinkled clothes that he's been there all day.

"*Hola, papá,*" I say, hoping my half-assed attempt at speaking Spanish will brighten him up. He nods in response.

Our chairs are awkwardly spread around the oval dining table, too far apart to make up for the missing fifth chair hiding in the garage. We sit in awkward silence, forks scraping against porcelain plates and mouths chewing chain restaurant Italian food. I break it by asking my mother to pass me the wine, this one a nicer brand of chardonnay.

"Are you sure that's a good idea?" Dad asks. It's the first thing he's said to me all day.

"Leave the poor girl alone, Manuel. She's twenty-one," Mom scoffs. When I pass the bottle back to her, she pours herself another glass.

"You're one to talk, Claire," he says quietly, eyes monitoring the rising level of wine in her glass. She doesn't respond this time, lowering her gaze to her plate. I do the same, trying to concentrate on eating the eggplant parmesan in front of me, but all I can see is 1060 calories, 54 grams of fat, 1990 milligrams of sodium, 113 grams of carbs—and Nina's favorite food that she can no longer eat. It's all my fault.

"I think I'm done," I declare, throwing my napkin on my plate and rising from my seat.

"You barely had two bites," Jesse points out, but I walk away before he can say anything else.

I walk into the kitchen and turn on the garbage disposal that's connected to the sink. I shove the remnants of my dinner down the drain, the loud growls drowning out my thoughts and concerned murmurs coming from the next room. Heavy footfalls sound behind me and I turn to see Jesse setting his plate on the counter.

"I'm fine," I reassure him, rinsing off the empty plate and setting in the dishwasher.

"Really?" he asks in disbelief. "You've lost, what, at least ten pounds since Christmas? Fifteen?"

"I've got it under control," I snap. I exhale sharply and close the dishwasher, leaning against the counter and crossing my arms.

"Do you?" he asks.

"Don't you have anything else to worry about? Have you even applied to Montgomery Community yet?" I counter, knowing the subject of school pisses him off. "Mom told me Foot Locker fired you. That was what, your fourth job this year? Maybe you should focus on keeping a job for longer than a month and actually doing something with your life besides playing Overwatch and smoking weed all day."

I know I've crossed a line, maybe even more than one, but I can't stop the words from flowing as I try to deflect the conversation to anything but me.

"Fuck you," Jesse spits at me. He drops his plate in the sink loudly, stomping out of the kitchen toward his room. I let out a sigh when I hear his door slam shut, rubbing my eyes with the heel of my hand.

Once I'm done rinsing his plate and putting it in the dishwasher, I walk back into the dining room to find Mom sitting alone. Dad's plate sits with his napkin folded neatly on top of it. Mom taps her nails against the base of her wine glass, eyes staring at the wall. She smiles at me appreciatively as I collect the plates, the corners of her lips curving up slightly, but her eyes still weighed down. It's all my fault.

I'm not sure how I became the most level-headed in our family. My need to have everything in order and my obsessive-compulsive tendencies kept me close to the edge in high school, nearly spiraling anytime something went wrong. But with Dad's quick temper, Mom's incipient alcoholism, and my brother's inability to do anything responsible, it seems as if I'm the top contender.

Jesse wasn't always such a slacker. He used to be incredibly motivated, always turning in homework on time and walking confidently anywhere he went. He was on his way to a track scholarship when Nina went missing. Something faded in him the moment the police showed up at our doorstep. I could see the motivation physically leave him. He's been slouching ever since.

After clearing the evidence of our family's failed attempt at a nice dinner, I make my way to Jesse's room to apologize when I see the door to Nina's room slightly cracked. I freeze mid-step, unsure if I want to keep walking or go inside. Unsure if I'm even welcome in her room. The door creaks open further, and I take that as a sign to enter.

The sight of her room hits me like a punch in the gut. Papers are sprawled across her desk, dried paint sitting in globs on a plate. I chuckle slightly at the sight—Mom used to hate when she did that. I step closer to it, picking up the half-finished drawings and watercolors. One on top, a painting of the view of the beach from our house down the shore, makes me tear up. The blues and greens are perfectly blended together, making the ocean look a lot clearer than it is. I can't even remember the last time one of us went to our beach house. It must have been years.

I filter through the papers, taking in her doodles of trees and flowers. I'm picking up a painting of a cat on a fence when my hand brushes something wet. I turn my hand over to see a streak of blue paint streaked from the bottom of my pinky to my wrist. I flip through the papers quickly until one catches my eyes. It's different from the rest of the colorful images, dark blue paint smeared across the page messily in three words: *Not your fault.*

With those three words, my breathing stops and my heart jumps into my throat. The world around me distorts and pauses, leaving me in a mess of colors and thoughts as I hear ringing in my ears. I reach to touch the paper with a shaky hand. It's all my fault. It's all my fault. It's all my fault.

The paint is still wet.

"What are you doing in here?"

My hand retracts from the painting instantly and the world resumes. I turn to see Dad standing in the doorway of Nina's room, instantly reminding me where I am. I see the repressed fury in his eyes, mouth scowled.

"Nothing, *papá*," I mutter, eyes glancing anywhere but him and around her room. Her bed is still unmade.

"I thought we agreed to leave her room alone?" he asks, eyebrows raised and voice shaky. "We don't need you coming in here and messing up her things. You've done enough already, don't you think?"

"Right," I scoff, my throat tight and tears prickling at the back of my eyes. I walk past him and leave the room without saying anything else, pretending I didn't see the tears he is holding in.

✦ ✦ ✦

It was no secret that my father loved Nina the most. She was the youngest, his little *consentida de papi*, willing to do anything if it meant spending time with him. I never had that bond with him, my unwillingness to learn Spanish as a teenager drove a wedge between Dad and me. He thought I was ashamed of our Mexican heritage. Maybe I was. The girls in my grade with their blonde hair and pink skin always made me feel jealous.

I never had a special bond with Mom, either. That was Jesse's role to fill. They would bond over the Eagles and cooking, him always desperate to help her in the kitchen any chance he got. She used to love cooking and trying new recipes each week, and I was always there to be the taste-tester for their creations. That ended when Mom stopped cooking and I stopped eating.

When I finally make my way to Jesse's room, I can hear the violent sounds of gunfire coming from his TV. He probably switched from Overwatch to something more violent like he always does when he's angry. Call of Duty, maybe? Grand Theft Auto? I can't tell the difference. I knock on the door loudly and the game he's playing pauses. He opens the door slowly; a frown covers his face when he sees that it's me.

"I'm sorry for being a bitch," I blurt out before he gets the chance to say anything. "My nutritionist has me on this low-carb diet right now and it makes me really irritable. Also, I... I worry about you, Jess."

His face relaxes slightly, and he opens the door wider, stepping aside to let me in. I walk past him and sit on the bed. My nose scrunches in disgust at the amount of food wrappers and Taco Bell bags scattered throughout the room.

"You need to clean in here," I say.

Jesse laughs. "Yeah, probably."

We sit awkwardly for a second, and I'm about to ask him what video game he's playing when he starts talking again.

"You don't have to. Worry about me, I mean," he clarifies when he sees my confused face.

I look up in surprise. "Yeah, I do. I clearly didn't worry enough about Nina and—"

"Stop, you know it's not your fault," he interrupts me.

"Dad seems to think it is," I say quietly.

Jesse shakes his head. "He's just hurting, and he needs an outlet for it, I guess."

"I thought work was his outlet," I say.

Jesse shrugs. "Maybe he needs more than one."

◆ ◆ ◆

Thirty minutes later we're all sitting around the dining room table again, only this time it's cake and ice cream in front of us. Mom lights the candles on the cake, a pink '1' and '8' representing how old Nina would be turning if she were still alive. We stare at the candles for a few seconds, but I'm not exactly sure what we're waiting for. My mother begins singing "Happy Birthday," and despite how creepy it is that she's singing for a dead girl, I can't help but chuckle. She's always been a terrible singer.

"Happy Birthday, dear Nina.... Happy Birthday to you," Mom finishes.

I look up to see Jesse repressing his laughter as well, the situation far too awkward for either of us to stay serious. We stare at each other, unsure if either of our parents are going to blow out the candles or if they expect one of us to do the honors.

Before we have to make the decision, a slight breeze rolls through the room, blowing the candles out. My brows furrow, knowing for a fact that all the windows are closed since my father thinks leaving them open is a waste of A/C. The radio in the living room switches on, and Patti LuPone's voice fills the room as *Don't Cry for Me Argentina* begins playing.

Dad jumps, his fist banging on the table and causing the silverware to rattle.

"Who took the CD's out of her room?" He asks sternly, eyes narrowing as they focus on me.

"Don't look at me!" I say. "You know I hate Broadway songs, why would I take the Av-eye-ta CD?"

"E-vee-tuh," Mom corrects me. She looks wearingly around the table, eyes flickering past Dad quickly. "Maybe it's Nina. You know, telling us she's okay?"

Dad scoffs. "Don't be ridiculous, Claire."

"I'm serious! Spirits have been known to contact loved ones before."

"Nina's dead," Dad says bluntly. He reaches forward, plucking the candles out of the cake haphazardly and cutting himself a piece. My mother continues to stare him down, Jesse glancing between them with raised eyebrows.

"I mean, it could be Nina's ghost. You know she always believed in that stuff," Jesse says.

"Don't encourage her, Jesse," Dad says sharply and Jesse sinks into his seat. Dad proceeds to cut pieces of cake for the rest of us, impatiently holding out a plate for me. I pass it down to Mom and he quickly places   another piece in front of me.

I glance down at my pink piece of cake. I can smell the sugar radiating from it; the strawberry scent permeating the room makes me nauseous. The brightness of the frosting almost blinds me, and I'm reminded of Nina's twelfth birthday when she wiped some frosting of a similar color on my nose.

I stand quickly, excusing myself to the bathroom. I immediately turn on the water after I close the door, splashing my face. My heart is back in my throat and my ears are ringing again. I feel my fingers tap against the side of the sink, the steady beat bringing me back to reality. I'm tempted to empty my stomach, to rid myself of the food I was fed earlier. Of the cake I haven't even eaten yet. Of Nina's favorite foods.

I shut the lid to the toilet loudly, sitting on top of it and throwing my head in my hands. I take my time, slowing my breathing, not wanting to return to the tension-filled table anytime soon.

My father is on his second piece of cake and my mother is on her third glass of wine when I return. I sit in front of my piece of cake, and notice a word written in frosting on the plate: *E A T.*

The ringing sound starts to return, but I shove it away. This isn't real. It's all in my head.

"This isn't funny, Jesse," I say, hoping he doesn't see it and that I've made it up.

"What isn't?"

I turn the plate around, sliding it across the table towards him.

"I didn't do this, Lyds."

He sees it. It's there.

"Well then, who did?" I ask.

"Maybe it was Nina's ghost," he says sarcastically.

"*Cállate,* Jesse!" Dad snaps. He grabs the plate from in front of Jesse and slams it down on the table, standing up. "I don't what kind of joke you all think this is, but it's not fucking funny. It's sick. Just stop it!"

"We aren't doing anything!" I defend, my voice raising as well.

"Why are you so against the idea of Nina trying to contact us?" Mom interferes.

"Because she's dead, Claire! She was murdered. It's time for you to accept that," Dad yells back at her.

"Stop it, Manuel," Mom hisses. "Don't fight. Not today. Please."

"Why, Claire? What does it matter? Eating some cake and ice cream and singing 'Happy Birthday' isn't going to bring her back."

"Where is this even coming from?" Mom asks, confusion clear in her voice and tears filling her eyes. "I thought we agreed to this. I thought we agreed to celebrate her birthday, to celebrate her *life*. I thought we were all okay?"

"*Okay?*" Dad asks sardonically, as if the word was painful for him to say. "Look at this family, Claire! All Jesse does is smoke marijuana all day. Lydia never comes home anymore and never fucking eats. You sit there and drink your fifth glass of wine of the night, acting as if you aren't completely shit faced. Who in this family is okay?"

Mom shrinks in her chair, head falling into her hands as she cries. It's all my fault.

"Stop it, Dad!" Jesse says loudly, standing to be on the same level. "Yelling at her isn't going to solve anything."

"Of course you'd pick her side," Dad scoffs. "You've always loved your mother more."

"Like you always loved Nina more?" I say before I can stop myself. I'm still sitting, and I look up at him with wide eyes. "Don't deny it, Dad. She was always your favorite. And you'll always blame me."

"No, Lydia, it's not your fault," my mother tries to lie to me.

"Why couldn't you have just waited!?" Dad snaps, interrupting my mother. "It was only an hour. Art club was only an hour. You could've just waited to drive her home."

His voice sounds so desperate that my heart breaks.

"You think I don't know that?" I ask incredulously. "You think I don't regret making her walk home? You think I don't remember every day that I could have stopped her from getting killed had I just waited for her?"

"Do you?" he asks coldly.

I want to scream at him. How *dare* he say that? How *dare* he assume I wouldn't do anything to bring her back? Before I can even argue, the lights begin flickering, then shut out entirely. The plate in front of Dad slides off the table, landing on the ground with a *crack!* as it shatters.

"See! It is Nina! She wants us to stop arguing!" Mom exclaims.

"God, Claire," Dad snarls. "Can you just stop?"

"No! Look, I'll prove it," Mom says. She moves away from the table, walking towards the open space between the dining room and the kitchen. "Nina, honey, is that you? Can you give us a sign?"

The lights flash on almost instantly, making my mother shriek in excitement. She turns to look at us, a wide smile covering her face and a wild look in her eyes.

"See I *told* you! I told you it was her!" she practically screams. She jumps up and down, crossing her hands over her heart. "Oh, Nina, I knew it was you. I knew it!"

"I told you to stop this!" Dad yells, but the music from earlier only gets louder, drowning him out. The lights flicker again, and I rise from my chair, joining Mom and grabbing her hand. I laugh in disbelief as the lights continue flashing and the album skips to Nina's favorite song from Evita. *Another Suitcase in Another Hall* flows through the room, and Jesse joins my mother and I with a look of wonder on face.

"This isn't funny! Stop it!" Dad screams over the music, his face turning red. "¡Para, por favor, para!"

With his last call for everything to stop, Dad's voice breaks, and the lights stop flashing. The music fades to an acceptable volume, becoming background music.

We look to Dad, pleading for him to believe us, begging him to just trust us this one time.

"I can't," he says. "I can't do this."

His face is streaked with tears and his breathing is heavy. He quickly walks away, leaving us alone with a half-eaten cake and melted ice cream. When the door to my parent's bedroom slams shut, the music shuts off entirely.

I look at what's left of my family.

"It was her! It was Nina!" Mom says desperately. Jesse wraps his arms around her, pulling her into a comforting hug as she continues to cry. His pained eyes look over her head and down the hallway where our dad disappeared. Whatever is left of my heart crumbles as I watch. It's all my fault.

◆ ◆ ◆

Later that night I dream of Nina. I see her walking through the streets of our neighborhood, the chilly March air nipping at her nose, a skip in her step as she hums a song from *Wicked.* I see a man stop her, asking if she had seen his dog. No, he asks her for directions. No, he doesn't even try to talk to her, he just grabs her. I want to yell to her, to scream at her to stay away from him and to run as fast as she can. I yell until my throat is scratchy and I can't talk anymore, but she doesn't hear me. I try to see the man as he takes her, but his face is blurry. He was never caught.

I see the police showing up on our doorstep two days after we reported her as missing. I see the captain's lips move as he tells us a body was found—one that matches Nina's description—but I can't hear him. I can only hear my mother scream as she collapses. I try to feel anything other than guilt and self-hatred and the house vibrates as Dad punches a hole in the wall.

It's all my fault.

I see Nina's funeral. I see her closed casket, her body too disfigured to be shown to the public. Her body is so disfigured that I can barely identify her at the coroner's office—a job left to me because Dad hasn't left his office and Jesse is taking care of our mom.

I see the world around me pause again. Nina's coffin opens and she sits up, dark brown hair healthy and shiny, blue eyes wide open and staring at me. She got them from our mother. I was always so jealous of them. I look around to see everyone frozen—our family, her friends, our high school teachers. I turn back around and Nina's out of her coffin, standing in front of me.

"Lydia!" she calls. Her voice sounds too awake, too full of cheer, like she just got back from a concert or a birthday party. I shake my head. This isn't real. She's not alive. She's dead.

She calls for me again, and even though she's right in front of me she sounds far away. I try to apologize, to beg for her forgiveness, to let her know I regret everything. She tells me not to worry.

"It was never your fault," she says.

It was. It is. It's all my fault.

"No," she reassures me. "You didn't kill me. You didn't do anything. It's not your fault."

She pulls me into a hug, and I can smell her vanilla perfume and strawberry shampoo. She comforts me as if she's the older sister, as if I didn't do anything wrong, as if she's not dead because of me.

I ask if it was her earlier in the dining room, if her ghost was there or if we were just going crazy. If we had shared psychosis. She laughs.

"I'm always there," Nina says, grabbing my hand. "I'm always with you."

She pulls away and walks back to her coffin and climbs in. I beg for her to not go back, to just stay here with me. She looks back at me one last time.

"I love you, Lydia," she says.

"I love you too," I tell her, but the coffin's lid is already closed.

◆ ◆ ◆

When I wake up, it's 3:33 a.m. I sit up in bed and run my hands through my hair. A cold draft blows through the room, making me shiver and look over to the window to make sure it's closed. It is. One of Nina's drawings is on the pillow beside me. It's the one of the beach views from our shore house. I'm not sure if Jesse put it there, or if Nina's ghost did, or if I grabbed it myself and just blacked out. I pick it up and carry it with me as I walk to the kitchen.

The house is completely silent; no sounds of video games or glasses clinking fill the air. I set the painting down on the counter and walk over to the fridge. I open it and the first thing I see is Nina's strawberry cake. Five pieces have been cut from it, my untouched piece from earlier sits in the middle of the container. I grab a plate, setting the piece of pink cake on it. I open the freezer and find the mint chocolate chip ice cream. I add some to my plate. I close the fridge and freezer, grab a spoon, and slide to the kitchen floor, my back leaning against the cool surface of the fridge.

I lift my spoon up. It hovers in the air as I look at the plate full of 543 calories, 31.4g of fat, 278mg of sodium, and 77.3g of carbs. I look at the plate of Nina's favorite foods. I look at the plate of strawberry ice cream and mint chocolate chip ice cream.

And I eat all of it.

It's not my fault.

✧ ✧ ✧

Paige Baselice is a writer based in Philadelphia, PA. She graduated from West Chester University with a B.A. in English in May 2019, and has since been working professionally as a copywriter. She grew up around the arts and she greatly enjoys live theatre and music. When she's not writing, she's either reading, cooking, or trying to find the nearest concert to attend.

7

WHITE PETALS*

R ani arrived at the Champagne Lounge of The Oberoi a half hour
early. She had chosen this as a meeting place precisely because Parnika
had likely never set foot inside one of Mumbai's five-star hotels.

She asked to be seated at a table that provided the best view of the
Arabian Sea. She wore a cream-colored Manish Malhotra sari and
ordered a whiskey, even though she didn't drink alcohol. Rani was
determined to do everything she could to set Parnika on edge. After all,
a journalist digging up the past couldn't be trusted.

Parnika called the day before. The two had never spoken before, but
Parnika shared that she was working on an article commemorating the
twentieth anniversary of the Bhopal gas tragedy. While visiting the
slums affected by the Union Carbide gas leak, she met Devi. The old
widow gave her a package to deliver to Rani.

When Rani hung up, she stepped out onto the balcony for air. She
hadn't heard from Devi in years. What had Devi told Parnika? Surely,
Parnika had not agreed to just be a messenger. She would want to know
her story. What web was Devi weaving now?

At five o'clock on the dot, she saw the hostess talking to a young
woman who she guessed was Parnika. As the hostess showed her to
Rani's table, Rani noticed the hostess gave Parnika a once over, a frown
appearing on her face.

But the young woman seemed oblivious, striding across the lounge
in her crumpled kurta and dusty sandals. As Rani shook Parnika's hand,

*Content notes: abuse, sex work

she felt her chest tighten. Choti, her younger sister, would have been her age.

When the coffee arrived, Parnika asked, "How do you know Devi?" Rani's hand wavered for a moment as she placed a cigarette between her lips. She lit it and blew a puff of smoke.

She planned to tell Parnika nothing, yet she found herself saying, "Devi was my neighbor. I lived in the slums until I was eighteen."

Rani watched Parnika slowly place her cup in the saucer. She guessed Parnika was trying to connect her leather handbag and designer sari with the slums she visited.

To Rani's surprise, Parnika didn't probe further. A serious look clouded the young woman's face. "Devi would like to see you. She's very ill. She's asked that you accompany me to Bhopal."

So, it was repentance. Rani shook her head. "I don't want to see her."

She crushed the cigarette in the crystal ashtray and signaled the waiter for the check.

Parnika drew a blue, velvet drawstring bag from her purse and placed it on the table. Rani swallowed, immediately recognizing it as her mother's. She felt Parnika's eyes on her, waiting for Rani to accept it. Rani looked at the young woman's hands, clasped as though in prayer. She caught a glimpse of a purple bruise on her wrist. She knew those kinds of bruises. Parnika must have noticed her looking because she quickly pulled down the sleeve of her kurta.

"Please reconsider," she said, leaning forward. "Devi doesn't have much time."

◆ ◆ ◆

Later, as dusk pulled a veil of stars across the sky, Rani stood on her balcony thinking about what she knew about the Bhopal gas leak. Weeks before it happened, she dreamed of a moon, blooming into a flower and spilling its white petals. They were four or five in the beginning and then they were twenty and then a hundred. They filled her chest and she couldn't breathe. She woke up with the knowledge of what was to come but couldn't tell anyone. Who would believe an eighteen-year-old girl's vision of an invisible gas that would kill thousands of people on a cold December night?

A week later, she was put on a train to Mumbai to work at a sewing factory. One of Devi's relatives had a tailoring business. He had gotten Rani a room at a ladies' hostel. Rani begged Ma to reconsider but she would hear none of it. With Baba's cancer treatment, their debts were mounting.

"Badi Ma has made all the arrangements, so there's nothing to worry about," Ma said, packing her bag.

Badi Ma, or Elder Mother, was a name Rani's own mother had given Devi, in honor of what she meant to Rani's family. It was Devi who held Ma's hand when Rani was being born. It was Devi who made kheer, Rani's favorite dessert, every year on her birthday. It was Devi who persuaded Rani's father to educate his daughters rather than marrying them off.

At the train station, Ma hugged her and whispered in her ear, *"Bhagwan teri raksha kare."*

But God had not kept her safe.

Some days, she could still smell the mildew in the brothel; she could feel the hot breath of men on her neck. The first few months in Mumbai when she couldn't sleep, she stayed up watching the sky, waiting for that moment when the dark bled into light, the sunrise being the only beauty in her life.

Then, she met Juhi, who'd been at the brothel the longest of any of the girls.

"You can't escape your karma, you fool," Juhi scolded, as she wrapped strips of cloth tightly around Rani's wrist to stop the bleeding. That was the first time Rani tried to kill herself.

After that, Rani accepted her life and things seemed to change. Juhi's boyfriend, Ricky, taught the girls to read and write English. He brought them little treats, Cadbury chocolate bars and milk barfi. He took them to Juhu Beach, the Gateway of India, and Malabar Hill, places in Mumbai far different from Kamathipura, the red-light district, where they lived.

One day, Rani was taken to a dance bar; it was one step up from the brothel. There, Rani was paid to dance and nothing else. She knew Juhi had a hand in this turn of her fate. When Rani went to thank her, Juhi winked and said, "Just don't let it get to your head."

Months later, the owner of the bar asked her to pack her things. Someone had seen her performance the night before and paid him good money for her. She moved from the cramped room she shared with three girls in Kamathipura to a one-bedroom apartment in Bandra where she lived alone. Every day, she was driven to an office where she learned to say "please" and "thank you," to eat with a fork and knife, and when she was ready, she was presented to her first client, Sunil.

✦ ✦ ✦

Rani emptied her mother's velvet bag on her bed. The sound of bells filled the silence in the room—it was her mother's silver anklet. She would follow her mother in the crowded bazaar, listening to the *chum chum* of her anklets so she wouldn't get lost. They were a wedding gift and the only jewelry her mother refused to sell for Baba's cancer treatment.

Rani checked the bag for the other anklet that would complete the pair, but it wasn't there. The single anklet was an invitation from Devi. Once again, she held Rani's life in her hands.

Rani fastened the anklet on her right foot. Bits of the past she'd kept hidden deep in her heart came spilling out. She heard Baba's gentle voice coaxing her to look ahead and not at the pedals, as she wobbled on the communal bicycle in the slum. She felt Ma's hands massaging warm oil in her hair. She heard Choti's eleven-year-old laugh, like a kite soaring in the open sky. Rani fell asleep, lulled by her memories.

When she woke up the next morning, she felt a deep ache for her family, something she hadn't allowed herself to feel since she came to Mumbai. She asked her driver to take her to the *Times of India* offices. At noon, she secretly followed Parnika to a crowded little restaurant. The man who met her there had black hair streaked with gray and wore dark glasses. Rani saw Parnika reach over to touch his hand, but he pulled it away.

For the next week, Rani followed Parnika. She lived in Bandra, in a bungalow overlooking the ocean. The tall walls of the compound were lined with barbed wire. Creepers climbed the marble trellises on the second-floor balcony. Every morning, Parnika rode in a Mercedes which dropped her off a few blocks away from the *Times* offices. She walked the distance, another face in a crowd of people on their way to work. In the evening, the car picked her up at the same location.

The following week, Rani read Parnika's articles on marginalized communities—house servants who raised their employers' kids, people with disabilities who started schools, and the untouchables who started their own businesses.

When she called Parnika to tell her she'd go to Bhopal, she heard relief in the young woman's voice. After Rani hung up, she opened her wardrobe and took out a slim vial from the safe. Juhi had pressed it into her hand as she hugged her goodbye the day Rani left the brothel. "Something to keep you safe," she whispered in her ear.

Rani held it to the light, watching the amber liquid slide from one end of the glass to the other. There had been many occasions when Rani could have used it, but it seemed as though fate wished for her to use it in Bhopal. She placed the vial in the front pocket of her purse.

◆ ◆ ◆

That night, Rani woke up with a start, her heart racing, her body drenched in sweat. Next to her, Sunil snored lightly. She put an arm across his chest, the solidness of his body returning her to the real world. She dreamed of white petals again.

The last time was six months ago. She had feared something happened to Sunil, so she called and texted him several times, but there was no response. Then he appeared on her doorstep a week later. There were dark circles under his eyes; he had not shaved in days and reeked of whiskey. His wife, Anjali, died in a car accident. Rani rocked him to sleep that night and every night until the light finally returned to his eyes.

A couple of days ago, he texted her just as she was going to bed. He needed to come over. So, Rani ordered Chinese from his favorite roadside stall, set the table, and lit candles. When he arrived, his grey hair was tousled, and his necktie loosened. Rani made him a Scotch on the rocks, which he quickly downed and motioned that he wanted another. He closed his eyes, taking in the Ravi Shankar music that she had put on for him. She saw the muscles of his face relax as his mind followed the path of the delicate tunes of the sitar. Then, he pulled her to him and kissed her hard on the lips.

Later, they stood on the balcony, smoking. A light breeze shifted the front of Rani's silk dressing gown. Sunil was an arm's length away from her and she could smell the musk on his skin, a scent she'd known for a long time. With her eyes, she traced the sweeping eyelashes, the graceful slope of his nose, the dip of cleft in his chin. He was lost in thought, miles and miles away from her. She knew better than to ask him what was wrong; he didn't want that kind of relationship.

"I'll be gone for a few days," she said, hoping he'd ask where she was going.

He simply nodded, his eyes not leaving the night sky. She would have told him everything, if he had asked. Waves of hurt rode up her throat and she excused herself, saying it was time she went to bed.

Rani knew by the time she woke up the next morning, he would be gone, leaving an envelope on her dresser. Over the years, the envelopes grew thicker, sometimes containing airline tickets to Tokyo or Sydney to accompany him on business trips.

During one trip to London, a pair of delicate glass birds in a store window caught her eye and on impulse, she picked them up as a gift for him. He accepted the wrapped box, but on the day of their departure, when she hurried back to the hotel room to get a forgotten magazine, she saw the box, still on the nightstand. She was heartbroken, barely able to speak to him on the flight back home.

In the weeks that followed, she took scissors to the saris he'd given her, the yards of silk transforming into a mountain of ribbons. She drank until she lost consciousness. But when he called, she never told him how she felt.

Now, she placed her hand over Sunil's heart and instinctively felt herself relax. In sleep, he was hers and that was enough.

✦ ✦ ✦

Rani and Parnika ended up taking the Punjab Mail train to Bhopal. The day before their flight, the airline workers declared a strike. They were lucky to have gotten tickets at the last minute.

As evening slipped into night, the lights in their train car dimmed. But Rani couldn't sleep. She remembered that, days after the Bhopal gas tragedy, Devi's letter had arrived. Rani hadn't heard about the disaster because she wasn't allowed television, radio, or the newspaper, but she already knew. For weeks, she didn't open the letter, refusing to accept the truth. She ended up tearing it to shreds, not wanting to read Devi's words.

Rani squeezed her eyes shut. Since then, she climbed the staircase of her life, moving further away from her past and towards the joy that being with Sunil brought her. At some point, she gave herself over to the soothing rattle and shake of the train and fell asleep.

A gentle touch woke her.

"Are you alright?" Parnika asked, helping Rani sit up. "You were crying."

Rani felt wetness on her face. Her heart was a wild horse in her chest. She had the dream again. Something was going to happen.

Parnika pushed a water bottle in her hand. "Drink," she said and sat down beside her. She pushed Rani's hair away from her face.

Rani first sipped the water, then gulped it down her dry throat. She sat back, hugging her knees. Both women sat quietly, listening to the sounds of the train: clang of metal wheels on the track, a muffled cough, tinny music from a radio turned down low.

Rani placed her hand on Parnika's arm. "Thank you."

When she saw Parnika wince, she quickly withdrew it. Then, she reached out and took Parnika's arm, gently pulling up her sleeve. Even in the dim light, she could see the purple marks.

"It's nothing," Parnika said, pulling her hand away. "I was ironing."

She reached over to open the window. The cool night air flooded the compartment.

Rani knew things about Parnika: the scar on her forehead that she covered with her hair was from a fall off a swing when she was a child; the indentation on the middle finger of her right hand was from her experiments with art. Large canvases with galloping horses and village women pounding grains filled the walls of her home. The one of the Mumbai skyline that she had given to her lover remained in its brown package in his office.

"I'm sorry about your family," Parnika's voice was quiet.

Rani lit a cigarette and took a long drag on it before turning her head towards the window.

"The article I'm writing is about the slum residents who helped the victims of the Bhopal tragedy. I call them 'Angels of the Night.' They took in orphans and cared for women who miscarried."

Parnika paused before saying, "Devi was one of those people."

Rani looked at the burning end of her cigarette. *What about my family? I'm an orphan because of her.*

"She had breathing issues because of the gas, but she still nursed people back to health."

Rani didn't want to hear any more. "I need some air."

She walked to the door of the train car and swung it open. She threw away her cigarette and stepped forward, swallowing large gulps of air.

It was all too much—agreeing to see Devi after years of throwing away the letters she kept sending her, going back to a place that reminded her of everything she'd lost, witnessing tragedies she could not stop. The black shapes of trees morphed into faceless figures as they whizzed by. The white stones lining the tracks glowed in the silver light of the moon. She stood for a long time, finally sliding down to sit on the floor as the wind whipped through her hair.

When Rani and Parnika reached Bhopal in the morning, they took an auto rickshaw to their hotel. Rani saw the city she was born in transformed by billboards and Internet cafes. It was different, yet familiar. They showered and ate breakfast. Rani thought Parnika would ask about the previous night, but she talked about the weather and where she had the best sticky and sweet jalebi.

When they arrived at the slum, Parnika led the way to Devi's shack. As they walked on the muddy path, children followed them. The elderly, perched on stools outside their homes, stared. Rani searched the curious faces, but she didn't recognize anyone.

Parnika stopped outside a shack. A young boy who followed them ran inside and soon returned with a young woman who wrapped a dupatta around her head. The woman smiled and nodded. She was Devi's helper, and motioned for Rani to enter. Later, Rani learned that she was an orphan whom Devi had raised.

As Rani entered the small space, she was struck by the strong odor of cooked food and unwashed bodies. There was a kitchen in the corner and just a few steps away, a sleeping area. How had she and her family lived in so small a space?

Devi lay still on a mat on the floor, her eyes closed. The young woman knelt and whispered something in her ear. Then she beckoned Rani to come closer and sit on the mat. Rani found herself unable to move. Anger sparked in her chest.

"*Namaste, béta*," Devi whispered, her eyes closed. Her face was a mix of brown and gray, as though the colors had run into one another on a palette of paint. Rani wouldn't accept *béta*—an endearment reserved for a daughter—from her, so she didn't respond.

"Sit," Devi said. Rani stepped forward slowly and knelt on the mat that was laid out in front of the bedroll. Devi was frail as a bird, but her manner was that of holding court.

Devi was like her. She realized years ago, when the congregation had gathered outside of a sick child's door. Rani and Devi's eyes met, and they knew. Though his fever broke, within days he was at death's door.

Yet, thousands had died that fateful December night. Neither she nor Devi had done anything to help.

"Why, Badi Ma?" Rani whispered, pushing down the tears that rose up her throat. She would not let Devi see her cry.

When Ma handed her the train ticket to Mumbai all those years ago, Rani looked everywhere for Devi to tell her about the dream, but found out she'd left for Allahabad to visit a sick relative.

"I wish I could have saved them all," Devi said, her voice like scraped metal. "I could only save you. That's the way it works."

"You think you saved me? Do you know what my life has been like? I should've died that day." Rani reached for her purse. With shaky hands, she took out the glass vial. In a moment, it would be over. The blood pounded in her ears like waves crashing on rocks.

The old woman turned her head, her eyes now open. If she saw the vial in Rani's hand, she didn't show it.

"What we have—what we know—can be a curse or a gift. It is how you look at it."

Rani shook her head. She had come here to settle a debt.

Devi's chest heaved, as though she were struggling for air. "Do not be afraid of the dream—act on it. The divination has a purpose. When you accept it, you will know who to save."

Then Devi began coughing. Her helper hurried inside. She lifted Devi by the shoulders, steadying her body with one hand, while the other rubbed the old woman's back. When the coughing subsided, her helper spooned water into Devi's mouth and laid her back down.

"Devi needs to rest now," the younger woman said. In the kitchen, she reached into a tall, steel container and pulled out a small cloth bundle. She placed it in Rani's hands where it rested with a small jingle.

When Rani emerged from the shack, she didn't walk over to where Parnika was waiting. Instead, she found herself on the path leading to the tin house where she had been raised. It was unrecognizable with posters plastered on the walls and a television antenna balanced precariously on one side of the roof. Two children played near the door. Time had marched on.

As she walked back, Rani turned the glass vial in her palm and threw it in a garbage bin.

✦ ✦ ✦

A week after returning from Bhopal, Parnika called with news that Devi had passed away. Rather than feeling satisfaction, Rani felt an emptiness, carved by the hate she held onto for so many years.

She continued having the dream, and each time she woke up unsettled, she calmed her panic, hoping that in acceptance, she'd find the answer she needed.

Then one morning, she saw Parnika's article in the newspaper. Halfway through reading it, she set the newspaper down. A knowing washed over her. *You will know who to save.* She picked up her phone and dialed Parnika's number.

Now, she stood at the ocean's edge on Juhu Beach. The setting sun cast a golden glow on the water. She breathed deeply, taking in the smell of the salty ocean and roasting corn from the vendor nearby.

Her phone buzzed. It was Sunil. He needed to see her tonight. She stared at the words on the screen for a long time, then put the phone in her purse.

In the distance, she saw Parnika walking towards her. Rani smiled and waved. Parnika waved back.

❖ ❖ ❖

Kalyani Deshpande was born in India and grew up in Zambia. Her essay, "Dear Mom Who Writes" was published in the anthology, *I Wrote it Anyway*. She was also a finalist in the NC State Fiction Contest. Kalyani works in technology and lives in the San Francisco Bay Area with her family. You can visit her website www.kalyanideshpande.com or follow her on Instagram @kalyani_writes.

8

MINERVA JAMES AND THE GOD OF STRANGERS*

The sound of a lamp crashing to the ground woke them. The groan of a man sounded from behind the guest bedroom door. Mrs. Fleur jumped out of her bed, followed by Mr. Fleur. They didn't even bother to put on robes, running in their pajamas through the dark hallway to the guest room. They tore open the door and were horrified.

The lamp, its ceramic body shattered on the floor, still flickered light from its bulb. The window to the second story room was open, a light breeze floating in. Sitting on the guest bed, next to the blood-soaked body of Sean Rosen, was their six-year-old foster child Lilly. Her hands gripped the butcher knife driven deeply into Rosen's chest. Her impassive expression betrayed not a drop of anger, terror, surprise. Lilly stared at her hands gripping the knife as if she was not sure what they had done.

◆ ◆ ◆

"How could a six-year-old girl have done this?" I asked, looking at the crime scene photos Minerva had handed me. The knife was nearly driven to its hilt into the man's chest.

"Ah, Mr. Robinson, your question seems to be the mystery in the case," Minerva responded. We sat in her office on the 10th floor of the building on L Street in Sacramento. In 1963, when this case was tried, the crime scene photos were still in black and white. The blood in the photos appeared as a black stain on Sean Rosen's body. There were also pictures of the girl, her hands dipped in blood, her face disturbingly void of expression. She had been wearing her pajamas when

*Content notes: violence

photographed, the small giraffes and elephants incongruously romping happily. The knees of the pajamas were stained in blood.

"I'm not sure a six-year-old could have physically done this," I said.

"I agree," Minerva said, paging through papers on her enormous desk. "But the police have little imagination. They believe that since the girl was found with the knife in her hands, the girl must be the person who drove the knife in."

"They're going to try a six-year-old?" I asked.

"In Juvenile Court. It's still an issue as to whether they can do so due to her tender years. But, as the Sacramento District Attorney told reporters, they just can't let her get away with murder, can they?"

I looked again at the photo of the expression on the child's face. Or rather, the lack of expression.

"This is spooky," I said. "Like something out of Alfred Hitchcock."

Minerva reached over and took the photos from me. She was a tall woman, nearly six feet, with carefully coiffed curly black hair. Her face, dark eyebrows and long patrician nose, held the stern beauty of a goddess. Today, she wore a pale blue blouse and a white bow. Her gray eyes regarded the photos again.

She sat back in her leather executive chair behind the enormous desk filled with files, books, and papers. On the corner of the desk sat 53 Cal Reports 2d, a case in that volume being bookmarked by a small black revolver. In the right corner of the office, the goddess Justicia stood on a small table holding the scales of justice in one hand and the sword of judgment in the other. To the left was a large window with a view of the Capitol building where my boss' namesake held court on the front portico.

"It is rather damning, isn't it?" Minerva murmured.

"Her hands on the knife are pretty damned damning," I said ruefully.

"Ah," Minerva said, "that is actually our one ray of light. But I did not call you in to give me your opinion of the forensic evidence, Mr. Robinson."

"Right, boss," I said. In my year of working as a private investigator with the goddess of wisdom, our relationship had comfortably settled into a Nero Wolfe-like dynamic: I conducted the interviews, she put the clues together and solved what needed to be solved. Because she was a criminal defense attorney—some say the most notorious in Sacramento in the early 60s—she had often lectured me that our job was only to find Reasonable Doubt, not to solve the mystery.

In cases like *In Re Lilly S.,* though, there didn't seem much room for reasonable doubt. When a girl is caught moments after the killing with her hands on the knife, there's not much wriggle room. Not even for a six-year-old. Minerva had been hired by the Fleurs to defend their foster daughter.

"What does the child say?" I asked.

"Not much," Minerva sighed. "In fact, nothing at all. She isn't speaking. Not to me. Not to her foster parents. Not to the police. Not even to the guards in Juvenile Hall where she's being kept in solitary confinement."

"That's not helpful," I said.

"It's actually quite intelligent," Minerva said, a slight smile playing on her lips. "I wish some of my adult clients had enough sense to stay quiet after arrest." She shuffled some papers and extracted two sheets of paper from the case file.

"Here are the people I need you to interview, Mr. Robinson. I would ask you to be careful but we both know that's unlikely, don't we? I only ask that you don't get yourself killed before you can help this little girl."

"Killed?" I asked. I was an Army veteran who had just come back from the then-unknown war in Southeast Asia. Minerva knew I could handle myself if things got dicey. "Don't they have the killer in custody at Juvenile?"

Minerva regarded me dubiously.

"Oh, Mr. Robinson. After our time together, one would think you'd know better than to make a comment like that."

❖ ❖ ❖

"He was a guest of ours, a stranger really," Mrs. Fleur said, showing me the scene of the crime. "Al brought him home that night for dinner. He was from an out-of-town firm which sometimes does work with my husband's office. He was working on a case in Sacramento and couldn't book a hotel because he got into town late. He seemed very pleasant for a lawyer."

I nodded as I examined the blood-soaked bed. When stabbed in the heart, blood spurts out like a fountain. Everything gets soaked. I took photos for Minerva.

"Did he say or do anything toward the child?" I asked. I took a photo of the bed, something the forensic guys hadn't done after the body had been removed. Mrs. Fleur had thoughtfully kept the bloody sheet on the bed. I could see the white space where the body had lain, surrounded by a sea of red.

"Nothing," Mrs. Fleur said. "In fact, when he came in, Lilly asked to be excused because she said she wasn't feeling well. Didn't even come down to dinner."

"You have another foster child living here?"

"Karen, yes. A teenager. Tragic, really. Her family was killed when she was staying overnight with a friend. Evidently, a burglary gone bad. Karen and Lilly get along like gangbusters."

"Did they know each other before?"

"I don't know. Lilly's father is dead. Her mother had a drug problem. Has, I should say. She can't seem to get off the heroin."

I shook my head. I'd seen my share of junkies in the jungle overseas. Heroin is a nasty beast that gets its claws in you and doesn't let go. I felt even more sorry for our little client.

"Do you know any reason why Lilly might want to stab a stranger in the heart?" I asked.

Mrs. Fleur shook her head.

"She's always been a quiet child. Every once in a while, she gets rambunctious, but not violent. She is very gentle with our cat. And our cat is a Siamese. Sissy, we call her. She doesn't take kindly to most folks. But she loves Lilly."

"How did Sissy react to Mr. Rosen?" I asked.

"She hissed at him and tried to attack his ankle. She didn't like him at all."

I nodded. To paraphrase W.C. Fields, a man who is hated by children and cats can't be any good.

◆ ◆ ◆

"I'm not gonna rat on Lilly, if that's what you're looking for," Karen said. She held Sissy as she spoke to me, almost as a shield. The Siamese cat's blue eyes glowed as if daring me to try to hurt the girl. *I would enjoy clawing you to pieces,* the cat's eyes seemed to say.

Karen was a large girl with mousy brown hair and green eyes. She had a button nose and rosy, chubby cheeks. But there was something guarded in her manner.

"I work with Minerva James," I said. "You might have heard of her. She's Lilly's lawyer."

"Oh, that's different," Karen said. She sat on her single bed which was draped in a pale pink bedspread. Posters of Bobby Vee stared down at me, hung with scotch tape on the wall. Elvis had fallen from the wall in the corner, forgotten in favor of the new god. There was a small record player near the bed, dresser drawers with socks and unmentionables draped across the top. And on the dresser, almost out of sight, a small photo of four people staring disconsolately out from eternity: Karen's family.

"Is it true what I heard? That Lilly might be too young to prosecute?" Karen asked, putting the cat on the floor. Sissy sat at Karen's feet and licked its paws, making sure I could see its sharp claws.

"My boss is looking into that. Six is a bit tender. But there aren't too many six-year-olds accused of murder, so we're in new territory."

"I hope they let her go," Karen said.

"They will likely put her in some kind of mental ward for children," I said. "They're unlikely just to let her go."

"That sounds horrible," Karen said, biting her knuckles. "Go ahead and ask me questions. I'll help any way I can."

"Has Lilly ever shown any propensity toward violence?" I asked.

"Lilly is six years old. What kind of violence could she show?"

"I'm looking for character evidence," I said. "Like Mrs. Fleur, who said Lilly was very gentle with Sissy. Siamese are not known as friendly cats."

"She loves that cat and that cat loves her," Karen said sadly, scratching the top of Sissy's short-furred head. "Sissy walks all over the house mewing, looking for Lilly."

"Evidently Sissy wasn't impressed by Rosen."

Karen smiled smugly.

"Animals know. They can smell evil."

"Rosen was evil?" I asked.

Karen blushed. She picked the cat back up and held it against her. After too long a pause, she said, "He was a lawyer, wasn't he? How can you get more evil?"

"Mr. Fleur is a lawyer."

"Mr. Fleur is a good man," Karen said. "He takes in foster kids that no one else wants."

"Why would no one else want you? You seem rather nice," I said, giving her a little flirty look. Standing six-foot tall, I had curly blonde hair and eyes so blue they were almost violet, just like Elizabeth Taylor's. I had no false modesty about my looks and was not above using them to loosen up a witness.

"Thank you," she blushed again. "But a lot of people would worry with a girl like me in the house. You know. *Her family was murdered. Maybe she did it.*"

"Pretty horrible," I said. "Did they ever find the guy who killed them?"

Karen pursed her lips and looked at the cat she held. The cat mewed back at her.

"No," Karen said quietly. "But I'm sure somewhere justice is waiting for him."

"What about Lilly?" I asked. "Why would no one want her around?"

Karen again pursed her lips. I gave her my best James Dean smile. She smiled back.

"Okay. Lilly can get…a little strange. Not just quiet. Unearthly. Then she'll throw things all over the place."

"Poor girl."

"That's why Mr. and Mrs. Fleur are my heroes," Karen said, scratching behind Sissy's ears. "They take chances with broken kids like us." She looked down at the cat and gritted her teeth. In a dark voice she hissed, "I wish that son of a bitch never came home to us."

✦ ✦ ✦

Mr. Fleur did not come home to be interviewed, so I called him at his office.

"Sorry, Mr. Robinson. I know you're trying to help our Lilly, but there's a crisis at the firm," he said over the telephone.

"Concerning Lilly?"

He hesitated.

"Sort of," he said. "Turns out Mr. Rosen was not a lawyer after all. We contacted the State Bar. There's no record of him. We called the firm he said he was with. They have no active case in Sacramento right now. And they've never heard of Mr. Rosen."

"Then why…"

"Why did he fake being a lawyer and ask to come home to dinner with me? Your guess is as good as mine."

✦ ✦ ✦

I reported these interviews verbatim to Minerva, who sat staring at a space above my head, her long elegant white fingers clasped together, her lips pressed against her hands. She said nothing for two minutes after I finished.

"I think I see," Minerva finally said. "But we'll get nowhere if Lilly doesn't talk to us."

"How do you propose to get her to talk?" I asked.

"I think I know one person who could break through."

✦ ✦ ✦

We sat in a private interview room at Juvenile Hall. Little Lilly, her curly blonde hair spilling over her blue jumpsuit, maintained a serious face as she sat at the folding table. The jail-issued jumpsuit was so big it nearly swallowed her.

Facing Lilly was a miniature version of Minerva. Like her mother, she had curly black hair. She had the beginnings of a long patrician nose and the lean body of a greyhound. But she also had rosy cheeks and a pair of sympathetic, sometimes mischievous blue eyes which she inherited from her late father.

Aphrodite. I knew from experience not to misjudge Minerva's ten-year-old daughter.

The two girls sat playing checkers. Aphrodite was giving Lilly a move here or there, but she wasn't letting her win easily. Aphrodite was trying to win a more difficult thing—Lilly's trust.

Minerva and I stood apart from the children, not even whispering. We perched ourselves against the wall of the interview room. Minerva busied herself with a court file so she could appear uninterested in the two girls' conversation. I closed my eyes as if asleep.

After half an hour of the game Aphrodite ventured a little small talk. What cartoons did Lilly like? What kind of ice cream did she like? How nice were Mr. and Mrs. Fleur?

Lilly gave monosyllabic answers. Aphrodite never pressed for an answer and kept playing the game. Lilly's reserve began to relax when Aphrodite asked her about her name.

"My grandma was called Lilly," the girl said. She sighed.

"It's a pretty name."

"You have a pretty name, too. Aphrodite? It's kind of funny, isn't it?" Aphrodite smiled.

"My mom gave it to me. She's named after a Roman goddess. Minerva. That's kind of a funny name too, isn't it?"

Lilly smiled.

"I've never met anyone with funny names like that."

"My name is from Greece. You ever hear of Greece?"

"A little," Lilly said.

"A long time ago they thought gods and goddesses controlled everything. The king of the gods was named Zeus. That's a really funny name."

Both girls giggled. I could have sworn dandelions sprouted in the interview room.

"What did Zeus do?" Lilly said.

"He was in charge of everything. And he was the god who protected strangers."

"Strangers?" Lilly stiffened. Uh oh, I thought. We lost her. But Aphrodite went on.

"Yeah, back thousands of years ago, Zeus said it was your sacred duty to take a stranger into your house and give him what they called 'hospitality.' That meant you had to be nice to him and feed him and give him a place to sleep. Even if he was your enemy."

"Oh," Lilly said in a small voice. Aphrodite made another checkers move but said nothing more. I've known veteran cops who couldn't handle an interrogation with as much skill.

"What if..." Lilly said, looking at the checkerboard. Aphrodite said nothing. She concentrated on her next move. Lilly looked up.

"What if the stranger was a bad man? What if the stranger was going to hurt the family he was staying with?" Her eyes grew intense. "What if the stranger stole a knife from the kitchen and he was gonna use it to hurt the family that he was staying with?"

Aphrodite regarded Lilly full in the eye.

"Then," Minerva's daughter said, "the stranger would break the sacred duty of hospitality. Zeus would hit him with a thunderbolt right in the heart."

"In the heart? That would be okay?" Lilly asked, her voice edged with a plea.

"Yes, Lilly," Aphrodite said. "That would be okay."

◆ ◆ ◆

"I don't know how you knew it," Lieutenant Holden said, "but Rosen's fingerprints were on the knife. Not defensive prints. It looks like he carried the knife intending to use it."

"You're being coy with me," Minerva said. We were sitting at the Lieutenant's desk at Sacramento Police. The hustle and bustle of the office was feigned. Everyone wanted to get a look at the notorious Minerva James. "Tell me what you found at Rosen's house."

"As you suspected, we found lots of stolen jewelry," the police officer said. "Jewelry connected to a series of burglaries where the occupants of the house were killed. Going back years."

Minerva nodded.

"I think you would agree with me, Lt. Holden, that whoever killed Mr. Rosen may have acted in self-defense. And defense of others."

"As you say, Miss James," Lt. Holden said. "I think we can also make some hay out of the open bedroom window, even if it was on the second floor. But I can't just let Lilly go. The D.A. would have a fit."

"Tell the D.A. that Lilly could not possibly have killed Mr. Rosen and you have proof."

Lt. Holden leaned back in his metal chair and folded his arms.

"Go ahead," he said. "I know you're about to pull a rabbit out of your hat."

"If Lilly had stabbed Rosen in the heart she would have been covered with blood. A heart punctured creates a geyser. Yet the only blood on Lilly's pajamas was on her knees. Meaning?"

Lt. Holden rubbed his chin. If he resented Minerva acting like a teacher, he didn't say.

"Meaning she knelt in the blood after the stabbing," Lt. Holden said. "That's why there was only an outline of Rosen's body in blood on the bed. Someone else stabbed him and ran."

"I'll expect Lilly released by morning," Minerva said, standing up. "If the D.A. has a problem, have him call me."

✦ ✦ ✦

"I have called the family in because I consider myself counsel for the entire Fleur household," Minerva said with a genteel tone, which brooked no argument.

They were sitting in a circle in the conference room on the tenth floor of Minerva's L Street office: Mr. and Mrs. Fleur, looking happy if bedraggled; Karen, dressed in a blouse and a modest wool skirt; Lilly in a pretty blue dress, sitting on Karen's lap.

I stood behind the Boss. She sat at the head of the table, wearing a blood red blouse. To her right, Aphrodite sat prim and proper in her Catholic School uniform. The child snuck a mischievous glance at me.

"We are grateful for all you've done," Mr. Fleur said to Minerva. He was a thin man, balding, with glasses. The very picture of a respectable lawyer.

"I haven't finished with this matter," Minerva said darkly. Lilly sat up and looked with concern at the Boss. Minerva nodded at her.

"Lilly, you've been a very, very brave little girl. But I, of all people, know that families have trouble if some are hiding secrets from the others. Remember, I represent you all. Whatever is said in this room is completely confidential."

Lilly looked around and caught Aphrodite's eye. Aphrodite smiled but it didn't seem to calm the other girl.

"I think we can all agree that Lilly could not have killed Mr. Rosen," Minerva said.

"She had her hands on the knife," Mr. Fleur said, ever the lawyer.

"Indeed. It is my theory that Lilly followed the murderer into the room, tripped on the lamp cord climbing onto the bed, and was trying to pull the knife out of the stranger when she was discovered."

There was an unearthly silence.

"That would mean that one of us..." Mrs. Fleur said in a quavering voice.

"True," Minerva said. "We could indulge in the myth that someone went in and out of the open window to the room. But I think we all know that this was a ruse by the killer that fooled no one—not even the police."

The Boss looked around the room waiting for a volunteer. None was forthcoming. She sighed.

"Very well, then," she said. "According to Lt. Holden, Mr. Rosen would get his victims to invite him into their homes to stay the night, usually with some ruse similar to the one he used on you, Mr. Fleur. After everyone was asleep, he would kill the occupants of the home and rob them of their valuables. There are numerous incidents going back years.

"When Mr. Rosen came home for dinner to the Fleur household, one person in the house recognized him. She'd seen him before. She knew him to be a killer because..."

"Okay," Karen's voice broke through. "Okay. I'll tell it."

Minerva nodded to her. The 15-year-old girl looked desperately at Mr. and Mrs. Fleur.

"When my family was killed, I wasn't visiting a friend overnight," the girl said. "That's a story I made up because I was scared. I was hiding in the closet because I'd heard screaming. I saw the killer walk by with a bloody knife. I was about Lilly's age then. There was nothing I could do to help. I was trapped. So, I hid. And he never found me. When he showed up for dinner last week..."

She shut her eyes. Tears sprung up. But she kept going.

"I knew him instantly, but he didn't know me. I had grown. I pretended to be nice to him. But I spied on him. I saw him go into the kitchen. I saw him take a butcher knife from the drawer."

She looked at Mr. and Mrs. Fleur.

"Karen, why didn't you tell me?" Mr. Fleur asked quietly.

"Would you have believed me? You would have said it was my imagination seeing killers in every stranger. And if you had caught him with the knife, he would have laughed it off by making some excuse. How could I take that chance?"

Mr. Fleur looked at the table. Mrs. Fleur began to cry. Karen continued her story.

"I knew I had to act after everyone had gone to bed. I told Lilly to hide. She asked why. I didn't have the time to make up a lie, so I told her that Mr. Rosen was a very bad man who wanted to harm us. I told her again to hide. But I guess she didn't."

"I wanted to help you with the bad man," Lilly said in a tiny voice. Karen drew her arms around the girl and smiled through her tears.

"I went into his room," Karen continued. "I went in without clothes, pretending that I wanted to seduce him. He smiled at that. Smiled! Can you believe that? I saw the butcher knife on his nightstand, and I knew what I had to do. I climbed onto the bed and grabbed the knife..." She took a deep breath. "I drove it into his heart as hard as I could. He looked surprised right before he died. I whispered my mother's name, but I don't think he heard it."

"The gods heard it," Minerva murmured.

"Since I wore nothing, I didn't stain any clothes with blood. I ran to the hallway bathroom to wash and put on my pajamas. I heard the commotion when the body was discovered. I ran in prepared to act shocked—then I saw Lilly."

"I was trying to help you," Lilly said in a small voice. "I thought if they couldn't find the knife..."

Karen wrapped her arms tighter around Lilly.

"My brave, brave little girl. I would not have let them convict you. I would have confessed. But when we hired Minerva...Everyone's heard of her. I thought she could get you out of jail."

"As I have," Minerva said. Did I miss something or was there the hint of a tear in her eye as well? Aphrodite, on the other hand, allowed her tears to run freely.

"Isn't it a weird coincidence that Rosen would come to the house where I was living?" Karen asked. "Of all the places in Sacramento, he came to the one place where he would be known."

"Not at all," Minerva said, clearing her throat. "It was inevitable, since the killer continued to prey on the same community, that he would eventually be discovered Also, the god of strangers could not, would not allow the killer's terrible violations of the oath of hospitality to continue without punishment." She shuffled a few papers on the table. "The police will say some unknown person climbed in the window and killed Mr. Rosen. Lilly was the unfortunate witness who will not talk and who tried to remove the knife thinking she could save the stranger. The case is closed."

Mr. Fleur was quiet. Mrs. Fleur rose from her chair and hugged both Karen and Lilly.

"I'll understand," Karen said quietly, "if you want to send me back to Children's Services. You can't have a killer living under your roof."

All eyes went to Mr. Fleur. An enigmatic smile played on his lips.

"My dear," he said, "the killer under our roof was justly executed."

"And his violation of the sacred oath of hospitality has been avenged. Zeus is satisfied," Minerva murmured. She stood up. "Thank you all for your cooperation. I believe our business here is done."

Mr. Fleur put his arms around his girls.

"Let's all go home," he said.

❖ ❖ ❖

Mark Bruce is a Vietnam-Era Disabled veteran who practices family and criminal law in San Bernardino, California. His first Minerva James story won the 2018 Black Orchid Novella Award. Five other Minerva stories have been published in such magazines as Alfred Hitchcock Mystery Magazine, Black Cat Mystery Magazine, and a few anthologies. He lives in Hesperia with Mariah the Mermaid and his support dragon Ferdinand.

9

SHAKSHUKA

Y ou're gonna love this place," Sam said over her shoulder. "It's a café with books in it. You like books, right?"

It would turn out to be the best meal Tamara ever ate. In a back alley of Jerusalem, before she knew how to navigate it on her own, before the guides for American tourists had directions to get to the doorstep of Adam's Café, Tamara was trying to step in the same place, on the worn stones that Sam had stepped on a moment before.

She'd only touched down in Israel two weeks ago. Like most American girls in the country, she was attending a gap year of seminary after high school, to be let loose in a country of unrest with nothing but an absurdly expensive phone plan on a cheap Nokia.

According to Mandy, a friend from back home who was attending a B-track school, Tamara's seminary was as low on the totem pole as you could get before actually reaching the bottom. You could still dip lower into the "rehab seminary" set, which was where parents sent girls they'd given up on.

"Your school," said Mandy, "is for the girls who put out." Then she realized what she'd said and tried to backpedal halfheartedly.

As far as Tamara was concerned, that was the least interesting part of her seminary.

Tamara's dorm was in the Har Nof neighborhood, an area that housed multiple seminaries. The students lived in five apartments on the same floor. The grout was dark in the corners and the showers rarely got warm. The girls were responsible for the cleanliness of their own apartments, which meant the common areas were in a constant state of disarray.

"Why are you here?" Sam asked on their first day. She stayed in the room across the hall.

"Because of my parents," Tamara said.

"No duh." Sam chewed a chapped lip. "Want some advice?"

"Sure," Tamara said, even though she didn't.

"Don't sign up for night classes. And don't take any of the small classes; they'll be able to tell when you skip. Unless it's your *machaneches*; those you have to take, and you can only miss two."

Tamara nodded. Sam reached towards her and for a second Tamara stiffened, certain that she wouldn't like what was about to happen. But Sam just took a strand of her light brown hair and rubbed it between her fingers.

"You're so lucky your hair is straight," she said. "And you can do a fringe bang. My hair does *not* like this water. But I guess that's partly my fault, bleaching it so much."

Tamara took the opportunity to examine Sam's platinum blonde hair, which looked yellowish. She couldn't tell if it was as bad as Sam said or if it was simply unwashed.

In the beginning, the other girls ignored Tamara for the most part. But their first Thursday night, just when the jetlag was starting to wear off, a British girl named Batsheva invited Sam to go to town, and Sam invited Tamara.

Technically, classes ended at 8:00 p.m. and lights were supposed to be out at midnight. She was embarrassed to ask if they'd be back in time. Then she reasoned to herself that there were four other girls, so that meant safety in numbers. It had been awhile since she was part of that large a number.

They hiked the inclines to the bus stop at the top of the hill. For fifteen minutes, they lounged around, trying to ignore Batsheva's loud singing. The other people waiting gave them a wide berth. When the bus finally arrived, they took over two sets of facing seats. Sam kept twirling around the pole in the center and flipping her platinum hair around. Then she complained she was hungry. The other girls ignored her.

Tamara's Hebrew wasn't stellar, but it seemed like no one's was. They got off the bus in town and Rivky, the short one, walked up to a trio of off-duty IDF soldiers.

"*Rikkud?*" she asked. "Dance? *Anachnu?*"

The soldiers looked uncomfortable, but one of them accepted her outstretched hand and started to slow dance. Tamara was instantly charmed. Rivky, however, looked bored. After the soldier spun her around, she let go and walked off down the street. The rest of the girls followed.

The soldier held out his arms and said something, to which Batsheva turned around and called back, "We're going to Underground later! Meet us at Underground!"

Sam fell into step next to Tamara and linked arms with her. "Show-offs," she said. "All of them."

Tamara didn't know what to say, so she just nodded.

"But not you, huh?" Sam concluded.

"Where are we going?"

"I don't know." Sam raised her voice. "Hey Rivky, where are we going?"

Rivky turned around. "Search me!"

They arrived at a dirty, sunken courtyard ringed by restaurants and bars just starting to light up in the dark. It stunk of beer and urine and feral cats. There was already a crowd of young people, all of whom looked to be non-Israeli students around their age. They just sat or stood and didn't go anywhere. They all looked hungry.

The girls settled at the foot of a large tree. Soon after they arrived, one of the bars started pumping disco music into the open air. Batsheva pulled out a pack of cigarettes. Tamara noticed the arrival of someone she didn't recognize—a cute petite girl with her hair half-up in a big bouncy ponytail.

"Who's that?" she asked Sam.

"Her? That's Dina, Rivky's girlfriend." Sam reached over and flipped Tamara's ponytail. "You'd look cuter with this down, you know."

Tamara shrugged. It was all she could manage, under the circumstances.

Eventually Rivky got up. The group continued to follow her lead, walking down a winding path at the edge of the square lined with bars and horny yeshiva boys. At the bottom of the road was another courtyard—the mess of smells quadrupled, made more confusing by a particularly potent sandwich shop on the corner—this one populated by people renting and smoking nargilas from a nearby stand.

A dark man in a soccer jersey and a sharp haircut set one up for them.

"Aren't they Arabs?" Tamara whispered to Sam.

"Uh, yeah," she said. "Maybe?"

Sam handed Tamara a small plastic nub wrapped in cellophane to plug into the hose of the nargila. It was surprisingly hygienic, especially considering that someone was getting a cartilage piercing ten feet away.

They sat on the low stone wall ringing the pit. Sam motioned toward the seat next to her. While Tamara could barely move the water at the base, Sam was able to draw the smoke in until bubbles violently shook the whole apparatus. The smoke, smelling of strawberries, obstructed Sam's face before dissipating up into the streetlights.

"Shotgun!" Sam said to her, before sucking on the hose and leaning toward Tamara abruptly.

Tamara jumped backwards, her body leaning away from the spot where their thighs almost touched.

"Will you quit doing that?" Sam said, smoke emitting from her lips.

"What ... what's going on?" Tamara said.

"If you stop running away from me, I'll show you."

Once again, Sam sucked on the little plastic nub in the *nargila*. The other girls pretended not to watch. Tamara fought to stay still as she watched Sam hold the smoke in her mouth, and then lean over again. She pressed her lips to Tamara's and gently blew into her mouth. When she pulled away, a lick of smoke seeped out between them.

"Blow it out," Sam said.

✦ ✦ ✦

The next day, Tamara could barely keep her eyes open. Visions from the night before kept appearing in her mind—images and sensations, as though the atmosphere was the only thing that would stick. A whirlwind with Sam at its center—the sweetness of her lips and a shred of undeniable confirmation that Tamara was as special.

Naturally, that was the day that Mandy decided to get in touch. She texted Tamara on and asked to meet her at the food court in the mall. Tamara agreed since her afternoon was mostly free—she'd only need to cut one class to make it.

When she got through the metal detector at the mall entrance, the harsh discord of the mall sent Tamara into a tailspin. The neon lights, the primary colors, the echoing accents of Hebrew bouncing off the high ceilings and mingling with the background Israeli muzak, intermixed like the smoke between their lips from the night before.

All at once, she intimately felt that she was an elementary school student in uniform, browsing for anime accessories. She was a new mother, looking tired but pretty, while her stubbled husband pushed their newborn's stroller. She was a middle-aged woman with bright burgundy hair carrying twenty plastic bags, meeting her friend for a walk around the amoeba-shaped perimeter. She was everything but herself.

Tamara wanted to live in that collectiveness for as long as it would have her. She could see other possibilities, infinity's worth of solutions to problems she couldn't parse before. She didn't want to be only one person, one path, ever again. She wanted her journey to end everywhere.

She walked around, too distracted by her surroundings to pay attention to her phone, and seemingly forgot all about her plans she made for the day, until someone grabbed her arm and her vision went momentarily blank. Through the haze, she heard Mandy's voice. Tamara took a couple of deep breaths, trying to find the equilibrium she'd felt a moment ago.

"This is so typical," Mandy said.

"Sorry. What? What's typical?"

"I'm keeping an eye on you like your mom asked and this is what I get. No good deed, huh?"

"I'm sorry. I'm sorry."

Once Mandy got over the insult of Tamara's tardiness, she led the way to a restaurant with a salad bar at the other end of the mall.

"Nothing is what I expected," Mandy said once they had their trays. "Everyone is on edge. I don't even understand what's attractive anymore—on guys *or* girls! Yesterday, I saw a girl in a tank top with bushes in her armpits! Did you know people like that even existed?"

Tamara averted her eyes.

"Have you taken on anything new?" Mandy asked, then barreled on. "I already wasn't talking to boys before I got here, so I think I'll stop watching R-rated movies. Not so hard to do when there's nowhere to watch them. Listen," she said suddenly with droll resolution. "Just stick to the rules and keep to yourself. Don't make friends with any weirdos. It can follow you for the rest of your life."

"You're friends with me, aren't you?" Tamara said quietly.

"What can I say. You're not *not* a weirdo, but that doesn't mean I'm not scared for myself."

Imagine.

Someone scared of her, a quiet girl with no sense of self.

Maybe it was the pain of having lunch with Mandy. Or the boredom of sitting through classes.

Or the intoxication of having no boundaries. Or, because when she'd gone into town with the other girls, Tamara had felt like she was part of a larger entity. Like the world was at their feet.

There were certainly catty arguments that threatened to blow out the windows of the dorm, of course. Rivky, especially, got into physical altercations with Batsheva with hair pulling and face scratching. When that happened, just when she belonged, Tamara felt a small part of herself retreat. It wasn't rage she felt; it was a lack of emotion. A lack of empathy.

And she was always keenly aware of Sam's location.

◆ ◆ ◆

About two weeks into the year, the jetlag had passed, and Tamara started waking up early. It wasn't intentional on her part—it was just that quiet times were few and far between, when she wasn't surrounded by students or strangers. Solitude was rare because she didn't know her way around the city yet. One morning, she sat in the common area, waiting for the day to start.

Sam appeared from out of her bedroom, fully dressed.

"What are you doing?" she asked Tamara. "Let's go out."

Sam didn't let her change, insisting she put her coat and boots on over her pajamas. Only when Tamara was being led to the bus stop, did she realize that no one else was coming. It was just the two of them.

She felt a little thrill go through her.

"Where are we going?" she asked.

"I want *shakshuka*," Sam said.

The town at 8:00 a.m. looked completely different from town at night. It wasn't seedy anymore, for one thing. The people who were out and about were a loud mix of jaded commuters and tourists looking to buy T-shirts. The sun warmed the Jerusalem stone and brightened the street until Sam led the way into a cool alley. Even the vile smells emanating from the corners were less threatening than they had seemed the last time they'd been there.

The paths looked like they might have landmarks, but Tamara couldn't differentiate them at all. They moved too quickly for her to translate any of the Hebrew they passed.

"How do you know where you're going?" she asked.

"I have a really good sense of direction," said Sam. She sounded bored.

When they finally reached Adam's Café, it was at the top of a steep flight of stone stairs worn smooth. The restaurant was just opening for the day. Wooden shutters, painted over a thousand times and still chipping, were being opened by a server with a long hook.

Sam led her through the arched doorways of the connected rooms to a couple of chairs by a small round table in a corner lined with books in Hebrew, English and French. Sam made herself comfortable and picked up a menu.

"How do you know about this place?" Tamara asked.

Sam ignored the question completely. She didn't speak, in fact, until the server came over and took their order. Tamara tried to think back. Had she done something wrong? Had she offended Sam in some way? But then again, everything Tamara had done was for Sam—everything at the whim of this girl. Tamara ordered the stuffed mushrooms and turned awkwardly towards the shelves behind her; she tried to hide how awful she was starting to feel.

"I told you you'd like this place," Sam said.

Despite the sentiment, Tamara still felt an unspoken disappointment from Sam, like she had taken a misstep somewhere. But why should that even matter? The fact of the matter was that Tamara was still reserving her opinion of the restaurant until after the food arrived, and the fact that Sam didn't know that made it even more of a crime that Tamara had ascribed so much to her.

Without warning, Sam smiled down at her phone. And then, abruptly, she was standing up, glancing toward the door.

"Going to the bathroom. Be right back."

Before Tamara could say another word, Sam was gone. Her sudden absence filled the room, shrinking Tamara down to the size of an iota. In an effort to appear occupied, she took down a travel guide from the shelf by her head and pretended to read.

At first, it wasn't clear that Sam wasn't coming back. But Tamara knew it, nonetheless. Though it felt to her like she knew Sam on an intimate level, they really had only just met. Certainly, they had shared the most intimate moment of Tamara's life. But this was effectively irrelevant.

Soon it was unavoidable: Sam was not coming back.

Tamara felt the edges of her vision begin to cloud as she faced this fact. She was alone? She was alone. In a strange city, in a strange country, with a language that was barely in her grasp. The tightness in her chest gave way to the undercurrent of emotion she'd been suppressing and, in a great crush of realization, she felt her cheeks color with the humiliation of it all.

The server approached with the coffee she'd ordered. Tamara dropped her eyes and tried to nod in quiet acquiescence.

Should she call someone?

There was no one to call.

It wasn't until the server returned with both orders that she realized she'd have to pay for all of it. She quickly calculated the amount in her head: just enough cash on her to make it, along with a paltry tip. If only she had left when Sam did.

But now there was a beautiful plate of mushrooms on the rickety table in front of her, next to a cast iron skillet with tomatoes, eggs, spices, and feta cheese that smelled like nothing she'd ever eaten before. It smelled like warmth. It smelled like care. The *shakshuka* also came with a loaf of whole grain bread and dips that crowded every available inch of the table. Everything in front of her was an invitation, asking for her attention.

Tamara switched to the seat on the other side of the table. She picked up Sam's fork and gently pressed it into one of the eggs in the *shakshuka*. She pierced it and the egg burst open, yolk running out in a gush, coloring its surroundings until it was absorbed by the rest of the dish.

After, Tamara walked along the cool stone alleyways on her own. When she reached the thoroughfare they'd crossed earlier, she looked up and saw that the street was full of people now, all talking and gesticulating, their faces lit by the morning sun.

❖ ❖ ❖

Alisa Ungar-Sargon is a Chicago-based writer. She received her MFA from Northwestern University. Her work has appeared in TriQuarterly, Lilith Magazine and JMWW, the latter of which was selected for Best Small Fictions and nominated for The Pushcart Prize. For more information, please visit her personal website at www.AlisaUS.com.

10

THE GHOST OF CHRISTMAS PRESENT

J aney leaned close to the mirror and, ignoring the stiffness in her hands, carefully stained her lips a soft, youthful pink.

Her heart fluttered. After weeks of counting down and careful planning, she'd see Landon tonight.

She smiled at herself. True, she had more wrinkles and sags than she did thirty-six years ago, but she looked better than most women her age. Plus, she'd spent almost two hundred dollars a few days ago to tone back her gray streaks and brighten the blond. Her nitwit of a stylist cut it way too short, but her daughter-in-law, Monica, assured her the hip pixie style flattered her. At this point, whether she agreed or not, she'd have to live with it. It just meant her outfit had to shine that much more.

She'd chosen a pair of black leather jeggings and ankle boots that women half her age couldn't pull off, and topped it with the V-neck leopard print sweater in grays and blacks that Monica had given her for her birthday.

This way, if her son, Tom, thought it was too flashy, she could say, "Your wife picked it out, after all!" and leave it at that.

Not that he usually commented on her clothes. Still, he'd seemed too suspicious by half lately when it came to her interactions with Landon, so she wanted to be ready.

Tom just didn't understand.

She fluffed her hair one last time and surreptitiously tucked the golden dice she wore around her neck into her ample cleavage. The charm warmed against her skin, a promise of things to come. Later tonight, she'd let it slip out so Landon would see it and recognize it. He'd know she'd worn it for him.

After all, hadn't they been doing this dance for the past two years since his wife passed? Hadn't Barbara told her to look after Landon? She was meant to do this.

"Jesus Christ! Aren't you ready yet?" She flinched as her husband's gravelly voice interrupted her reverie, then her fist clenched at her side.

Goddamn Robert. He wasn't even supposed to be here. He should be in the goddamn hospital, but those goddamned doctors cleared him in time to send him home for Christmas. She'd hoped they would keep him a few more days after his pneumonia so she could have a break.

Plus, with him in the hospital, Landon might have picked her up and driven her to Tom's himself.

"Shut up, you miserable ass! It's Christmas. Unlike yourself, I want to look good in pictures." She grimaced at his navy fleece vest over a blue plaid button-down.

Robert grunted and shook his head, revealing a patch of silvery strands amongst the dark gray. She was certain they hadn't been there before his hospital stay.

"Let's go, then," Janey said.

As he led her through the hallway toward the foyer, it struck her that he hadn't even said she looked nice. Typical.

"Geez. Is there anything left at the store?" Robert pointed toward the four carrier bags overflowing with wrapped gifts for their granddaughters. Without waiting for a response, he grabbed three of them and started for the car. His usual ruddy complexion looked bluish.

She didn't waste her breath suggesting he take it easy so soon out of the hospital. His stubborn ass would insist he felt fine. Instead, she focused on the remaining bag. She nibbled her lip, wondering if she should've buried it.

But no. Of course, she would bring Landon a gift. Nobody expected her to go empty-handed. It was Christmas, after all, and if she didn't give him something, it would be rude.

She'd been careful with what she'd chosen, though. She'd thought and thought about it. It had to seem unassuming, casual, practical even, but it had to be more. It needed to tell him what he meant to her, what they could be together, to whisper at intimacy.

"Do you need me to come get that one, too?" Robert called to her from the car.

"No, no. I've got it." She lifted the bag of remaining gifts and locked up, clutching his gift to her chest like a warm hug.

In the car, she stared out the window, tuning out the drone of the news broadcast that saved her from having to talk to Robert.

◆ ◆ ◆

They'd been married for less than five years, but when Janey thought back on them now, they were the most exciting years of her life.

From meeting at a party, to their whirlwind romance while he finished college, to the way he whisked her away from her small-town existence and showed her another world, Landon had thrilled her. She and Landon ate at fancy restaurants, partied with friends, and traveled with his family. They'd been young and carefree together.

Until they had Tom, and she'd had her car accident. Things unraveled. They divorced.

She'd met Robert at a bar one night not long after. She needed a father for her toddler, and Robert needed a mother for his three teenagers. It made sense.

But it turned out Robert worked a lot, so she got stuck at home with four kids. Then Robert's ailing mother moved in with them and remained for several years until her death. Janey might as well have been his live-in housekeeper than his wife.

Even during his time off, he didn't "waste" money on restaurants or traveling. Instead, he saved it. Because nothing was worth buying. His idea of a vacation was spending a couple hours at the Jersey shore before returning home the same afternoon.

When he retired early, she got sick...but she tried not to think of that. Her cancer was in remission now—at least she assumed it still was; she hadn't bothered going to the oncologist in years. What was the point? So, Robert could resume taxiing her back and forth to appointments where doctors could give her bad news and more pills? No thanks.

At first, she hadn't thought much about Landon. Not until she found out from her ex-sister-in-law that Landon lived with a woman named Barbara. Then Janey mulled over all the fabulous adventures Barbara and Landon must be enjoying together, all the trips to New York and long weekends in Nantucket, all the laughs they shared while she was stuck with Robert.

So, she befriended Barbara—called her, made conversation about Tom growing up, swapped funny stories about Landon. It became easy keeping tabs on him that way. Sometimes when she called, he'd pick up and talk to her a few minutes before passing the phone to Barbara. Those were her favorite days.

They did that for nearly thirty years until, two years back, Barbara found a lump. "I worry about Landon," Barbara confessed to Janey before she died. "I don't want him to become a hermit. You know how he can be. Look out for him, would you?"

She had Barbara's blessing. Barbara knew—had always known— Janey and Landon belonged together, could be happy together.

Janey knew it, too. After all, they'd been such great friends when they were married before, hadn't they? Plus, they had a son together. True, that son was grown now, but the history was there; the connection established. Reuniting would be as easy as sliding back into your favorite pair of warm slippers.

It would be perfect.

◆ ◆ ◆

He was late. So late.

Though she'd managed to chew and swallow the food on her plate, she tasted nothing. *Where was he?*

She affected indifference even as Tom and Monica discussed his absence and goddamned Robert finished his second helping of pork. Guess his appetite returned.

"Look, I talked to him four hours ago and he said he'd be here," Tom said.

"Yet, he's almost an hour and a half late! Even worse than last year. How hard is it to be punctual? And when he gets here—*if* he does—

he'll take his time eating as if we all aren't waiting on him. His thoughtlessness drives me nuts." Typical Monica. She never gave Landon the benefit of the doubt about anything.

Janey cleared her throat. "Maybe you should call him, Tom?"

"Mom, I called him three times. It keeps going right to voicemail."

Oh God. What if he didn't come? He *had* to.

Then, miraculously, as though her Christmas wish had been granted, the front door opened, and he appeared. She let out a relieved sigh.

"We were starting to think you weren't going to make it," Tom said.

"I got turned around on one of the roads and went left when I should have gone right."

Janey knew the feeling.

He stood, unsmiling, under the arch of the kitchen, dressed in dark-washed jeans, a black sweater, and loafers. His silver hair could use a trim, but she didn't mind it that way. The man had always had great hair. She wanted to continue drinking in the sight of him, but Monica's sharp, unwelcoming words interrupted.

"Well, you'd better eat then. The girls are ready for the main event."

Landon, as oblivious to Monica's annoyance as he was to his grandchildren, sauntered to the table.

By the time he sunk into his seat, the girls were out of theirs and running around the kitchen. "When are we opening presents?" they chanted.

"After everyone has eaten. It'll be soon." Monica shot a pointed look Landon's way. He didn't notice that either.

Robert rose from his spot at the table and shuffled to the living room, the girls following him as though he was the Pied Piper. At least he was good for something.

With the decibel level noticeably diminished and Robert out of the way, Janey leaned forward to hear Landon blaming the GPS for getting him lost. She let her finger dip into her shirt to pull the necklace outward. She manufactured a laugh and watched as Landon's gaze swiveled in her direction.

She willed his eyes to discover the dice charm. "Didn't you used to tell me, 'You're not lost unless you're out of gas'? Remember that trip we took to Maine one Christmas? We made so many wrong turns I didn't think we'd ever arrive, but you kept assuring me we were fine so long as we had gas in the car."

Before he could respond, Monica said, "Well, those girls are going to run out of gas if we don't get to the presents soon. Eat up, okay?" Landon's attention slid away from Janey and back to his salad.

That bitch, Monica!

Still, Janey had to admit she was looking forward to the gift exchange as much as the girls were.

Landon had been wonderful at buying her presents when they were together. Money was never an object, and he usually bought whatever glittery gem she'd pointed out to him, or her favorite perfume, or boxes of expensive chocolates. Even last year, when he'd come to Christmas dinner for the first time in decades, he'd given her luxury hand soap. Which seemed appropriate so soon after Barbara's passing.

But Barbara had been gone a full year now. In that time, Janey telephoned Landon several times. He'd asked her to help him choose a new sofa this past summer and go Christmas shopping more recently. She made the mistake of mentioning both invitations to Tom who considered Janey shopping with Landon "inappropriate and awkward," and ended up taking Landon himself. She wondered about Tom sometimes. What son didn't want his parents to be together?

At least Landon did.

That's why she had spent months fantasizing about this year's gift.

She knew when it was time, it would be rife with possibility and hidden meaning, just like her gift to him. She closed her eyes in anticipation.

Landon took his time eating his meal, ignorant of the angst he caused.

In desperation, Janey fiddled with her necklace. The pendant made a sawing sound as it moved along the chain.

"Mom, are you wearing *dice* around your neck?"

Janey sat up straighter. She could kiss her son for giving her an opening. "Yes, I am."

Tom's brows furrowed. "Why? Have you and Robert been hitting the casinos without my knowledge?" He laughed.

"Of course not. You know Robert never wants to go anywhere! No, Tom, these are almost 40 years old."

She let the significance of the timing linger, fixed her gaze on Landon, and waited for him to connect the dots. Landon squinted in her direction but said nothing.

"Your father bought them for me. Do you remember, Landon?"

He cocked his head to the side, and she held her breath as she watched him place the memory. "Oh right. You picked them out that time we took a cruise with my brother. We spent the night in the casino, and I was on a winning streak at the craps table—"

"—Right! I was your lucky charm! You didn't start winning until I stood next to you."

She pretended not to notice Tom's pinched look as he shook his head at her. Instead, she focused on Landon who, strangely, mirrored his son's movement.

"You know I never believed in that nonsense. It's a game of odds, Janey. And I increased my odds of winning when I started betting smarter." Still, he stood up and walked toward her, positioning his wire-rimmed magnifiers on the edge of his nose and reaching out to inspect the bauble. "I'm surprised you still have this; it's not even real gold."

He straightened, letting the charm thud against her shirt. She winced.

Her granddaughters, noticing Landon's movement, fluttered back in. "'S'it time for presents now?"

Tom stood. "Yes! I think it's time."

Janey was almost breathless. It *was* time.

✦ ✦ ✦

The living room looked like a Toys R Us had exploded. Shreds of wrapping paper spilled out of bags, while Monica and Tom struggled to free dolls from their plastic prisons and snap together flimsy castles destined to break within days. Robert and the girls retreated downstairs to the family room to work on a puzzle.

"The girls have so much energy, don't they?" Janey said to Landon as she sat down next to him on the sofa.

"They're awfully loud."

"Sometimes, yes. But I promise this is nice and quiet." She handed Landon the gift she'd special-ordered for him.

He opened it, revealing brown, wool-lined leather slippers. They were warm and cozy and looked just like the pair she'd bought him their first Christmas together decades past. "Does this mean you promise to always have my slippers waiting for me when I get home?" he'd teased her that day. Today he said, "Oh good. The soles just gave out on my old slippers."

Before she could react, he added, "I guess I should give you your present now."

Her heart pounded. She couldn't wait to see what he'd chosen for her. Jewelry was out of the question, of course. She was married. And perfume would be too obvious. Still, some gourmet truffles from Lawson's would be acceptable; nobody but the two of them would realize the history there.

"Oh? You didn't have to get me anything..."

He waved her off. He'd never had much patience for social niceties.

"I left it out in my car."

"Should I...do you want me to go with you?" she asked, a burning feeling growing inside her stomach.

He blinked at her. "No, that's okay. I'll be right back." And he walked out of the house toward the car she imagined might carry her away from this place, back to the life she should have been living this whole time.

◆ ◆ ◆

She thought about the past few weeks. Hell, the past few decades.

Robert was a mistake. So, what if he'd carted her to doctor's appointments for years? Big deal that he'd provided financially for her and Tom, or that his grandkids loved him. There was more to life than that.

"Mom, you have some pretty selective memory," Tom said to her recently, while he drove her to the hospital to visit Robert. She'd been reminiscing about how exciting her life had been with Landon. "Things with my dad weren't that great. You told me story after story back then. About how he wasn't around or supportive when you were together, especially after your crash and during your recovery. How he'd been resentful at the responsibilities that fell on him while you laid in a hospital bed for a month, both your legs in casts and your jaw wired shut. About how he didn't even give you child support after you left him, and we both know he never took any interest in seeing me. Honestly, if Barbara hadn't passed, we wouldn't be hearing from him now."

That Tom had such an active imagination.

Moreover, Tom didn't understand. She could have it all again. With Barbara gone, Landon was all alone. He'd need her. And Robert? Oh, screw Robert. Enough of her life had been wasted with dull, miserable Robert. Didn't she deserve some happiness finally?

✦ ✦ ✦

The door clicked as Landon returned holding a rectangular box, larger in all dimensions than an ordinary shirt box. This kind of box could contain only one thing: a robe. She knew it to her core. And after she'd gotten him slippers, it couldn't have been more poetic.

He'd bought her a robe! Would it be plush and cushy, the kind she'd cuddle into on cold winter nights? Would it be thin and waffled, the kind she'd slip on fresh from the shower? Maybe it would be a terry cloth. Red, of course, because he'd remember she had one when they first married. But no matter what the style, a robe spoke of intimacy, a promise. It was more than she'd dared hope for.

"Well, here you go." He placed it on the table in front of her. "Do you know they do gift-wrapping at malls now?"

She tingled all over. Her lips curved into a smile as she removed the shiny gold bow on top and slid her finger under the rich green paper embossed with holly leaves. Although she wanted to tear through it, she restrained herself, savoring the moment, gently detaching the inch-long rectangular tape along the paper's seams.

When she reached the brown box underneath, she glanced up at Landon.

This moment. She wanted to remember it forever. The past was behind them. So many lost Christmases. But now, in this moment, the tide would turn. This gift would seal their future. She took a deep breath, staring at Landon even as she removed the lid, pushing aside red tissue paper, memorizing the crinkly sound it made, like the flapping of angels' wings.

Finally, she let herself look down.

She blinked. Then blinked again.

The box housed twelve vibrant lemons; each yellow teardrop nestled in a bed of green tissue paper.

She blinked a third time, as though the act might change the sour fruit into the robe she'd been expecting.

Landon craned his neck to peek inside. "Ah. So, you got the citrus box. I couldn't remember which was which. There's another one in my car that has pears and nuts, if you'd prefer that one."

She forced herself to answer him, her voice a near-rasp. "No, no. These are...fine. Thank you. They look..."

Monica's sudden appearance saved her from having to come up with a tactful adjective to describe the gift. Janey willed her arthritic hands to close the lid before Monica spotted the contents. But they, like the rest of her, had frozen, immobile.

"Ooh, what do you have there?" Monica peered around the newly-assembled Barbie car she held. Her forehead furrowed.

The buzz of Landon's voice blathering to Monica about the practicality of edible gifts filled the space around them.

"Right. Well, Janey, let me know if you need some recipes to use those up. If all else fails, you can make lemonade."

Janey fake-laughed at her daughter-in-law's snarky comment, but before she could say anything more, Landon flitted away. Settling on the opposite couch next to Tom, he struck up a conversation about a documentary he'd watched on his streaming video service.

"That Landon. What a guy, huh?" Monica grunted. "I'm going to give this to the girls," she added before leaving Janey alone.

◆ ◆ ◆

Landon continued talking to Tom for twenty excruciating minutes. Janey attempted an occasional interjection, but Landon barely paused to acknowledge her.

When Robert and the girls finished their puzzle, he dutifully began loading his and Janey's gifts into their car.

"You ready?" he asked after his second trip.

Was she?

She looked to Landon, hoping once more for a signal, for some indication that he was masking his intent from the attention of the rest of the party.

"Do you need me to get that one, too?" Robert asked her, pointing at the now-closed box on the sofa next to her.

She stood. "Yes, thank you. It's a bit too heavy for me."

After bestowing hugs on their granddaughters and Monica and Tom, they left. Landon didn't even stop talking long enough to say goodbye.

The temperature seemed to have dropped several degrees from the time of their arrival. The night air bit at her cheeks and her feet ached from her stupid ankle boots.

"I warmed up the car for you. Hurry and get in so you don't catch anything."

Robert took his place behind the wheel.

Her body on autopilot, Janey turned to follow his direction, but stopped beside the row of black trash bags lined up against the garage. Next to them sat the box from the red wagon Landon gave the girls as a present. Like the bags, it overflowed with paper, ripped to shreds and crumpled into deformed balls, the ugly aftermath of once lovingly-wrapped packages.

Standing over the box, she reached inside her coat and gave a sharp tug. The cheap old chain broke and slithered down her neck. She listened to the clink of metal as the dice clattered to the bottom of the trash heap.

When she climbed into the passenger seat, Robert turned to her.

She looked at him, his face ruddy from the cold, his glasses slightly foggy from the warmth in the vehicle. "Let's go home," she murmured, "I'm tired."

Robert nodded and put the car in reverse. Janey reached forward and flipped on the news.

She stared out the window, focusing on the drone of the broadcast that saved her from thinking of the box of lemons on the seat behind her.

◇ ◇ ◇

Natalie Monaghan Munroe has been writing stories since the third grade. What began as overly dramatic diary entries and serialized tween dramas has become overly detailed baking blog posts and steamy women's fiction. In between writing book-length emails and texts to friends, she earned a BA in English Literature from Rosemont College and a Master of Education from Arcadia University. Natalie is the mother of 2 daughters, 2 cats, and a puppy, and is happily married to her biggest fan. She loves coffee in the morning, tea in the afternoon, cookies anytime, and daily workouts to even it all out. Her cooking exploits can be found at www.nataliemunroe.com and her random musings on Twitter @NatalieMonamun.

11

THE BEST YOU

You were so shy when we first met, sitting alone in the corner of the café reading Bradbury. I asked you if you'd finished the one where all of the astronauts' dreams come true. You said you had, but that you thought it was a sad story.

"Why?"

"Because," you said, "their dreams destroy them in the end." Your shining brown eyes darted away, before slowly returning to meet mine. I sat down beside you and asked your name. You were so nervous, chewing on your collar and biting your thumbs. I can still remember the chestnut color of your hair, the round shape of your face, the bright singsong intonations of your voice. I loved who you were then.

We started spending all our free time together, pouring our moments into one another, sharing our meals and our secrets. You showed me the color of your soul and I showed you mine. Then we began tracing the lines of each other's bodies with the tips of our fingers. That was when I found the mole at the base of your spine.

"Be careful," you said.

"Why?"

"If you press it, I'll change."

"What?"

"The mole, if you press down on it, I'll change into another person."

"What are you talking about?"

"Stop! Don't touch it."

"Sorry."

"It's okay," you said with a sigh, resting your chin on my chest. "I don't know how else to explain it. It's where he touched me before he...left."

"Who?"

"It doesn't matter. He's gone now," you said, turning away from me. "It was a long time ago. All I know is that if you press down on my mole, I'll change. I'll become someone new. Someone different than who I am now."

I lay there listening, silently contemplating what you said.

"Do you like me the way I am?" you asked.

"Yes, of course."

"I've been this way for a long time. I've felt safe in this skin. But now that I have you, I'm not afraid. I trust you. I'll become whoever you want me to be."

"I like you just the way you are."

You looked at me again, smiling big, and kissed my face. "Good. I just need you to know that if you ever do press it, and I do change, I can never go back to who I was before. Never again."

Lying there, I ran my finger down the length of your spine towards the mole. I circled it with the tip of my finger. "I love you," I said.

"I love you too."

It would be an understatement to say things changed after that night. I couldn't stop thinking about your mole, all the possibilities. It poisoned my mind. I started to look at you differently. Traits I once adored became irritating. I no longer found your coy demeanor endearing. Your ankles weren't slender enough. Your laugh was too high-pitched. And all of these insecurities sprang from the same thought, the idea that I could make a better you. What if it were possible? What if you could make me happier? What if you could become someone I'd loved even more?

It was only a few days later, as we lay in bed, that I slid my hand down the length of your back and pressed the mole. The change was instantaneous. It was jarring too. Especially that first time. It wasn't just the change that shocked me, but also what you changed into—an infant, no more than a few weeks old. I had no idea what to do with you.

You were lying on top of me, plump and naked, nuzzling my chest. I cupped your tiny head in my hand and turned you over onto your back. Your hair was softer than flower petals. I wiped the drool from your puckered lips and watched you scrunch your fingers and kick your pudgy legs in the air. Your eyes lit up and your mouth widened into a little 'O' when you saw me. That's how I knew it was you. I felt like you wanted to tell me something, so I sat there with you awhile, listening to you coo and cry.

I was nervous though. I felt unprepared to raise you on my own. I was also worried that this might happen each time you changed, and that I'd be very old by the time I found the version of you that I'd imagined. So, I lifted your backside gently off of the bed and pressed your mole.

Now you were old, more than twice my age. Your skin sagging, wrinkled, marked with liver spots, your thin gray hair cropped short. You closed your eyes and took in a deep breath, then, smiling, said, "I can smell you. Come to me, I want to touch you."

And I let you touch me, and I saw your milky eyes searching. You were blind, but you put your hands to my face, felt my skin, the structure of my skull. You saw me, and I kissed you.

You were frail in form, but your hands were strong and your spirits high.

"The key to aging," you said, "is preservation. The flowers of youth may wilt and die, but the honey endures with safe keeping. Savor every moment."

And savor the moments we did. Even blind, you made your way around the kitchen with ease. I watched you stuff zucchini flowers with ricotta. You motioned for me to come over and we both took a deep inhalation, taking delight in the aroma of herbed cheese.

"Life is all about the spices," you said, taking my hand.

We made love after dinner. You were so aware of your body, how to make the most of each motion, every touch. There was so much you could show me. We lay in bed for a long time, talking about life. You knew so much.

We spent several days together, me and that version of you. "There are still so many things you need to experience," you said. "You can't waste your youth on me." And we both agreed that this was not the best version you could be. Not for you. Not for me. So, I kissed your wrinkled cheek and pressed the mole again.

A redhead, short and curvy, bright green eyes, young, sultry, ready to roll. You smelled of lavender and I breathed you in. You hugged me, your plush cheek against my chest, your fiery curls tickling my neck. You stepped back, looked up at me, and said, "You're kind of cute, for an older guy."

You were so vivacious, so sassy. "Let's go dancing," you'd say, or "Let's go to that new restaurant," or, "Let's go see that movie," "Let's go to the show," "Let's move to Paris!"

You talked so fast, jumping from one thing to the next, dancing around the kitchen in your high heels. It was hard for me to keep up with you, keep your attention. You were always looking at your phone, posting pictures, texting your friends. I'd ask you what you were doing, and you'd tilt your head to one side, dig your fists into your hips, and narrow your eyes at me. I'd feel silly for having asked. Then, you'd let out a sharp laugh.

You loved to laugh, to curse, to drink—wine spritzers, beer, tequila shots, and whiskey. I was drunk on your youth, your beauty, and the alcohol. I let you get away with whatever you wanted.

We'd go out dancing twice a week. It was fun, but I hated the way other men looked at you. They wouldn't leave you alone, always asking for a dance, if they could buy you a drink. You'd laugh off their advances, but I was still jealous. I was greedy for you, lustful. Our bed was on fire—our bodies burning with booze—but I was nervous that you'd leave me, that you'd find someone more attractive, someone more interesting, someone new.

"Do you like this version of me?" you'd ask.

"Yes," I'd lie, and you'd give me that look, where you'd tilt your head and narrow your eyes at me. I didn't want to let you go, but the anxiety was killing me. After you fell asleep one night, I kissed the soft skin above your shoulder blade and pressed down on your mole.

After that, I became indecisive. I'd flip through versions of you like I was watching TV. Too fat, too skinny, too old, too young, too uptight, too introverted, too talkative, too timid, too tall, not tall enough, too needy, too sick, "Does this thing come with subtitles?"

It didn't matter what version of you appeared, none of them were good enough. Some would stay a few days, others less than a minute. I'd always find a flaw, often in simple or silly things; the color of your hair, the shape of your nose, what brand of shampoo you used. I developed a sort of apathy about the whole thing. I'm not sure who was more exhausted by it all, me or you.

Then I found a version I liked. You looked more like the original version of yourself, only a little taller, your ankles more slender, your gaze steady, your laugh hearty and deep. Your chestnut hair was darker, espresso, and your brown eyes were a golden flecked hazel. You could tell by the way my face went slack that something was different.

"What is it?" you asked. I was speechless.

You didn't chew your nails the way you used to, but you still loved to read. The books were different though, instead of literature, you now preferred science. Behavioral psychology was your passion.

Given our situation, this newfound interest proved to be valuable. Our discussions started with Maslow and progressed to Jung. We'd discuss the different iterations of you we had created, which characteristics were most desirable, and the least.

Finally, you asked, "Do you like this me?"

"Oh my. Yes," I said.

"What is it?"

"It's just so simple. You're so…regular. You could be anyone."

"Oh. That is good. Isn't it?"

"It is. So good."

We both agreed. And we folded ourselves into one another, believing our words, joining our souls. This was the best you.

We'd talk about ourselves constantly, openly. We would articulate our emotions, discuss them, try to find ways to improve who we were. We'd do laughter therapy at the breakfast nook, walking meditations in the afternoons, journaling at night. With your encouragement, I even started exercising regularly. The best you was making an even better me.

We were so happy. We made love each night and afterwards lay in bed talking, planning our future together.

"We should get married."

"Really?" you said, scrunching your nose.

"What, you don't want to?"

"No," you said, with a teasing smile as you wrapped your arms around me. "I do. I want to have your babies."

That never happened. After speaking with the doctors, we found a flaw in the best you, you could never have a child of your own. We visited a few specialists, but there was nothing to be done. And just like that, our happiness dissipated.

You were so sad. The light in your eyes was gone, and no amount of positive psychology could change that. I tried my best to comfort you. I'd bring home books on adoption and we would lie in bed at night looking at pictures of all the children that could be ours.

"It's just not the same," you'd say.

We both knew we had another option. With resignation, I placed my hand on the small of your back. We pressed our lips together and I pressed my finger to your mole once more.

It was never the same again. I'd lay there next to these other versions of you thinking of the sound of your voice, the way you'd whisper good morning in my ear. I was angry all the time; my finger ached from the constant repetition of pressing your mole. I'd scroll through the different iterations with abject disgust. None of them were as good as the best you.

You were tired of it too. I stood in the kitchen with the latest model, long limbed and dark skinned, your eyes lulling. You were so weak, I was practically holding you upright. I hung my head. You knew what was coming, so you hugged me, resting your hands on the back of my neck. I sighed and pressed the mole one last time.

Then you were gone. I was dumbfounded at first. I looked all over the house, in the closets, under the bed. I looked all over town, at the places the different versions of you had liked to go. Restaurants, bars, cafes, the movie theater, the library. You were nowhere to be found.

That night, I lay awake, alone, in what used to be our shared bed. I couldn't stop thinking about you. I couldn't sleep. I was trying to make sense of it all when I realized the truth. We were wrong about the best you. The best version had been the first one. The bookish, shy girl from the coffeeshop, the one with chestnut hair that chewed on her thumbs and looked away when she talked. The one I fell in love with. That was the best you. It had been all along.

And I wept as I thought of all the different versions of you I'd created in an attempt to find something better. All the laughter, hardship, and meaningless love that we shared. I reflected on each iteration of you, the ones I'd fancied, the ones I'd ignored. I thought about the last you, how sad and tired you looked holding me in the kitchen. I wished I could feel your touch again. I reached for the last place you touched me. There, on the back of my neck, I found a mole. I circled the strange lump of flesh with the tip of my finger. I pressed down on it. I pressed hard.

Adam J. Newton is the curator and organizer of the Bucks County Writers Group. He made his authorial debut in the 2019 collection of short stories, Creaky Stairs, A Book of Dark Truths, contributing seventeen pieces of original fiction to the collection, including: Lilies of the Field, Chong's Garden, the Better Left Alone series, and The Spring House. The latter was adapted into a short film of the same name by filmmaker Bruce Logan and featured in the Best of Local Haunts Film Festival in October of 2020. Adam lives in Bucks County with his family and beloved Shih Tzu, Minima.

12

LILITH'S FLIGHT*

*I*n the beginning of one world, the earth was the Mother and from Her body God made the plants, trees and flowers, shrubs and vines. He made the animals, the insects, the fish and reptiles, and sent them roaming across Her surface. Then He dug deep into Her mud and fashioned from clay the curves and lines of a human. He split this human down the middle into two parts; a woman and a man, named Lilith and Adam.

They blinked their eyes open and gazed around them at the lush heart of the garden of Eden, all that they needed within their grasp.

Lilith and Adam walked on new feet, ate of the garden, and looked up with new eyes at the wide blue sky.

And when Lilith turned to Adam, she saw a part of herself standing beside her.

The garden was surrounded by a high wall to keep paradise in and to keep the wild world out.

This is yours to enjoy, *God said, gesturing to the garden all around them.* But only if you do as I say. I am the Father, *He said. The Almighty. You are my children. To you I speak my name of power. And He did, and it shimmered above them in the air and beat against their new hearts. I am what I am, He said. A name you must know but are forbidden to speak.*

✦ ✦ ✦

A woman was made by the hands of her father and the culture that formed him. He molded her woman's body to be slim and pliant. He told her that he held her name, he knew her worth and it was measured by him and all the other men that were to come.

---

*Content notes: sexual assault

When she'd been a girl, she had run with the boys, raced them on bikes, her long hair flying, tangling behind her, her body a tool of her own adventure. But when the marbles grew beneath her chest and the hair began to sprout between her legs, the words used to describe her suddenly changed. Her body was no longer hers, but a tool of others.

When a teen, she had rested her school bag on the damp grass of the oval and surveyed the surrounding crash of teenage boys in their ill-fitting growth, limbs long and skinny, faces uneven and pimply, voices loud, breaking in air. She saw the threat in them, the promise. Those who would decide who she was.

Her father had taken to calling her cheap, had warned her that boys only ever wanted *one thing*, had wrapped his thick fingers around her throat like a collar.

She found a boy who wanted her, who told her she was beautiful, who made a nest in his arms for her to be safe from the others. He said he loved her, whipped her in the face with a sock for fun, kissed her eyelids, and told her she was a whore.

And she was insatiable for him. She was every word they said she was, her body waiting to be filled, named, tasted, molded and made real by their hands. And each time she was told she was loved, she understood more deeply that hate and love were the same thing.

The girl grew to a woman. She lay in bed in the dark beside the boy who was now a man. There had been love as she understood it, now rusted, dissolved in parts, powdered to reveal the sharp twisted edges beneath. She stared at the ceiling with a rock inside her where a heart should be. She heard the man turn over towards her and she swallowed and stopped herself from turning away.

He was there so close. A body she knew better than her own. He reached over, grabbed her breast like a doorknob and squeezed hard.

You never want to do it anymore, he said like she was withholding a prize.

Please don't. I'm tired.

There was silence while she waited for him to let go, turn over and swallow his hate, but he was silent, his fingers digging deeper into her tender breast. Then his hand was between her legs.

Please don't.

He had taken her many times while she slept, and reported in the morning how easily he slipped inside her limp body, the act so elicit that it took only two, three strokes to be done. She felt only air where her boundaries should be.

He'd never taken her while she was awake, never when she could speak and feel and say no. But that night, he pulled down her pajama pants to her knees and crawled on top of her.

Her hands met like a prayer to push against his chest. He gathered her thin wrists in one hand and lifted and held them above her head while he arranged himself with his other.

His hands, her hands. Above, below.

All the words of the world peeled away when he entered her. Her skin shrunk and wrinkled like wet paper. There it was. The serpent slithering, the whispering beast within him, without permission within her.

A new language had been spoken in her ear. She was made again, molded in his image.

She lay silently while he pumped and used her body for friction, his eyes closed. The serpent spoke for him. The world squeezed against her chest.

In and out while she breathed, or didn't breathe, until in silence, finally, he pulled out of her like a sigh. He deposited a sacred pool on the valley of her stomach that filled her navel.

Then he let go of her wrists, her hands still crossed and limp above her head. He rolled onto his side of the bed, snuggled down, and breathed into sleep.

In the dark, on her side, the whole world had changed. The edges sharp, the size of her shrunk, and her soft skin turned to rot. The cups of her ears caught shedded tears. She shivered as she pulled tissues from the box beside her to mop up the semen that sat on her skin like a slug.

The next day, she was silent, wary and woken. She observed him as the predator, she, the prey. At a party that night, she watched from a distance him laugh and joke with others, one hand gesturing, one clasping his beer. She held her own hands in front of her body in confusion and looked for some difference in him, some sign that a line has been crossed, that a life had been broken, that a beast was silently breathing in him, but he would not look at her. When their song came over the CD player, long and lilting and full of yearning, she waited for him to turn and see her, to be seen. Instead, he called to someone else and walked past her to hug them, his body fully his own.

She went home by herself and lay in the dark.

In the morning, he was back beside her.

Do you still love me? she said to the man like he was every father, every man, every wound, every cruelty.

His voice was flat. *I don't know.*

She nodded. *You need to go,* she said, like she had spoken her own name for the first time.

And he did.

✦ ✦ ✦

Every day, Lilith and Adam woke side by side upon a soft bed of moss and stretched their arms into the air.

Will you lay with me? Adam asked one morning and gestured to his swollen penis.

Lilith groaned softly; her body ripe like fruit. I will gladly lay with you, she said and reached forward to hold him by her side.

Lie beneath me, he said.

I will not, *she replied.* I am your equal, we were both made of the earth.

I am the heavens, you are the earth, Adam said.

I am heaven and earth, *she said.* I lie beneath no one.

✦ ✦ ✦

Years passed. The man and the woman sometimes saw each other. When they did, there was a hunger in her that he took for desire. She knew he was there before he walked in the room. He stood close and her skin tightened because she heard his serpent whisper, and felt the heat of him. When faces were turned, he touched her body like it was still his to take. And she let him because he'd remade it in his image, and she still felt no claim. They knew each other, had seen the shadow in the night, knew what hid within their bodies and lives beyond.

Sometimes she thought of the night he took her and what was taken, but only as a story of her worth, a story of her making. Only as the clay figure already formed that had a small hole widened by his body, widened and split up the middle like a new design.

Eventually, there were other men with other hands and serpents—their weight pressed upon her, their ribs against her stomach, her body beneath theirs. And she was still hungry, hungry, but always there was the ghost of the man beside them. Still his handprint on the woman's skin like a branding. His rib, the framework of her body. Her life, an afterthought, something tacked onto the end of a more important story.

The man sometimes called her on the phone, and she would answer, heart beating. One day, phone pressed to her ear, she heard a hiss filled with secret words he couldn't hear. Beneath the hunger, she discovered there was a grief that could tumble out if she let it, a pouring pile of unspoken words heavy enough to bury him.

When she hung up, she stepped to her mirror to look at the body she had worn but never claimed. Her skin began to crinkle and gather in soft ripples across the surface, the hair of her head sprouting strands of silver.

She gathered the rolls of her stomach into her hands, fistfuls of soft clay, then got into her bed and lay flat. Nothing pressed upon her but layers of quilting, her own hands beneath, mapping her surface like a stranger. *Tell the truth*, it hissed, hungry all over again. *Tell the truth.*

◆ ◆ ◆

When she next saw the man and his hand touched her side, the grip felt tight and cold and unknown. Later, she tried to call him, the hiss gathering, but the number rang and rang and when the voicemail kicked in, her lips pinched white.

She texted him. Asked him to hear her. He replied that he would. Said, *you're family*. But when she called again, he didn't answer. And when she sent messages, he no longer replied.

A fire gathered within her, her outside edges curled back singed. She sat on a rock and wrote a long message to him about a young man and a woman in the dark, of a hand on a breast, of the weight of his body upon her. The words spat from her in text, each letter propelled from a place hidden and carried from one age, one stage, one relationship to another. With each word she was lighter, her fingers fast and true, the bones and skin of her body remade and claimed her own.

She sat in the sun when she was done, her finger paused over pressing Send. The world was calling. She pressed the glass of the screen and closed her eyes, the earth suddenly wild and open.

✦ ✦ ✦

Adam told God that Lilith would not lie beneath him.

God told Lilith to obey. She had been made to please Adam, to be subordinate to him, to stop him from mating with beasts, God said.

Lilith looked upon God and smiled, teeth bared. I am subordinate to no one, *she said.*

You will be punished, *said God.*

I know your name, *said Lilith.* I know the name none may speak, and I speak it. I am what I am, *she said.* I am what I am.

Banished, *said God.*

I go, *said she.*

✦ ✦ ✦

The man got out of his car and the woman got out of hers, leaning against the side with tremoring heart, trembling hands.

After all we've been through, he said, voice gathered in accusation.

She looked at him squarely. All those years ago, *she said.* I said no, you climbed on top of me and did it anyway.

His eyes narrowed and he turned away. He walked stiffly down his driveway without ever looking back.

I am what I am.

She could feel the size of her bones.

✦ ✦ ✦

Lilith spoke the name that none must utter and made it her own. The power of that name gathered like a rising wave within her.

God was angry, but the rage of God meant nothing to Lilith as the wave rose, her neck lengthened, her fingernails narrowed to claws, her shoulder blades sharpened, protruded, then fanned out in feathers. Her body made of earth and clay and stars.

Outside the garden was bush and vine and bramble. Forests and hollows, mountains and valleys. The voices of the underworld called from below. She stepped forward, looked back at the garden, Adam cowered near the tree with God blazing beside him.

We'll try again, *God said to Adam.* We will fashion a new woman who will not say No. This one will be easy. Forget that night hag.

Lilith walked forward, picked a path where there was none and ran, ran, her body leaping, wiped clean, no handprint. Her new wings shot forth, dark and wide, and pumped and bellowed, lifted her higher and higher and propelled her forward on her way to her first horizon.

Samantha Benton is a writer focused primarily on the complex hidden stories of women. She has been published in numerous Australian literary magazines, but these are her first words to travel over the ocean. She is a library professional living on unceded Wurundjeri land in the tree covered hills of Melbourne, Australia with two of her three grown sons. Visit her website at SamanthaBenton.com.

13

Between Strangers

Most of the basement of Blessed Sacrament Church was dim, but its kitchen was bright, and Sarah's eyes adjusted to the bluish fluorescent fixtures glowing on the Formica counters and linoleum floor. She hung her coat and scarf on a hook near the door, shivering a bit, then turned the wall oven to 350 degrees, eager to warm the room, and unpacked her groceries.

Sarah often cooked in the kitchens of friends and family because her tiny apartment kitchen was practically useless. She was used to the stress of searching in drawers, asking others, "Where is your cutting board?" or "Could you find me a peeler, please?"

Now, she was alone in the quiet basement, aware of her clanking and breathing, as though her body and actions reverberated in the space. She tiptoed. In a lower cabinet she found a large stockpot, filled it with water, and put it on the stovetop with the burner on high. She opened a small bottle of Diet Coke from her grocery bag and sipped.

"Sarah?" A voice surprised her from the doorway.

"What? Yes, um...hi," Sarah said to the nun peeking in from the dark hall.

"Hello. Sorry to startle you. I'm Sister Ann Marie. We spoke on the phone?"

"Yes, hi. How are you?" Sarah put a saucepan she had been holding onto a front burner, smiled, unsure if one is supposed to shake the nun's hand.

"I just wanted to say welcome, and see if you needed anything before I went up to the service."

"Um, no, I'm fine, I think." Sarah was trying to remember if she had seen a nun since her third-grade teacher. She was suddenly embarrassed of the rhinestone stud in her right nostril. "And thanks again for letting me come down here early. My little apartment..."

"Oh, it's no problem." Sister Ann Marie waved her off and smiled. "We appreciate the help. The family does." Sarah nodded. "Well, I'll be up in the church if anyone needs anything. Please let Gayle know when she arrives."

"Sure, yes. Thanks." Sarah relaxed her shoulders as Sister Ann Marie left and laughed at her nervousness. With the heat low under the saucepan, she unwrapped a stick of butter to drop in. She swirled the butter, watching it slowly puddle in the warm pot. "What the hell am I doing here?" she mumbled, digging in a drawer, as quietly as she could, to find a whisk and a scraper, happy to find a silicone one.

Sarah had called Gayle, the head of Blessed Sacrament's Altar-Rosary society, to volunteer to cook for parish funerals. Her mom had said, "It'll do you good, get you out of your apartment for something besides work. And you love to cook, don't you?"

"But what should I cook? And I won't know anyone. They won't know me."

"Sometimes that's best," her mom had said. And in that, Sarah heard her mother's continuous disappointment, her disapproval, her fear that there was no one left in town who thought Sarah was normal, was good.

So Sarah called Gayle, her breath tight, unsure what this might entail. "It's just something I can do—cook."

"Thank you, Sarah. We'll be in touch," Gayle had said.

When, two days later, Sarah received a call that there would be a funeral, she was surprised. She felt like a volunteer firefighter, rising to action, responding to a crisis. It seemed such a grown-up thing to be doing. A responsible, respectable thing. She began paging through recipes in her mind. Maybe she could double her grandma's raisin spice squares, dotted with walnuts, drizzled with orange icing. Or a large sheet of brownies would be good, without nuts because the kids wouldn't like them, and dusted with powdered sugar. But she didn't want there to be too many desserts. She should make something more substantial. Her favorite chicken Dijon would cost too much. She could not imagine what these strangers would want to eat at a party for the death of someone they loved.

Now, with the church bells resounding upstairs, she was worried about what she would do when the families arrived, what state they would be in. She hoped they would not be crying, at least not dramatically. A few somber tears she could handle, tears calmly whisked away with convenient tissues, maybe with faces directed toward the corner of the room. She could handle a woman quietly staring, poking at her plate of Jell-O salad, eyes welled. But she didn't know what she would do if there was wailing, and weakened women crumpling their devastated bodies up against their men. She hoped she could busy herself in the kitchen undisturbed, unnoticed.

Sarah heard footsteps in the hallway, assuming it was Sister Ann Marie again. A man's voice called quietly this time: "Hello, is this where Mike Yoder's funeral is?"

She turned to see a man in his thirties in a black suit and wool overcoat. "Um...yes," she said, "I mean, I think that was the name." She wiped her hands on a dishtowel. "But the service is in the church. The lunch here is not 'til after the...um, after the burial."

"Oh." He looked at his watch and stood for a moment. Sarah wondered why he hadn't seen the cars near the church, latecomers walking in. She opened a plastic baggie of minced onions and stirred them into the melted butter. They sizzled gently. He said, "I must have gotten the time wrong. Time zones and all." She stirred, wondering why he didn't leave.

"The service is still going on. You can just head up." She peeked in the stockpot—tiny bubbles covered the bottom. She sipped her Diet Coke.

"Well, I could..." he took a few steps around the kitchen and peeked in a cabinet, its hinges creaking. "I mean, um...would you need any help down here?" Something in his voice was hesitant, lonesome. Sarah felt he needed to stay. She had thought, when she had first arrived, that she would prefer to be alone, but now that he was here, she did feel a bit more at ease. Having someone there dispelled the dreamlike quality of the over-bright, echoing basement.

"Sure, I guess," she said, reaching for a plastic baggie of flour she had brought. She stirred it into the saucepan. "I mean, I'm just making one thing. Other ladies will come and drop things off, but…"

"Okay, good." He hung his coat, stood near her, feeling the countertop with his hand before leaning against it. "Rob," he reached for her hand.

"Hi then, Rob. Sarah." She put down the scraper and shook his hand limply, quickly, then back to stirring the foaming roux. The nutty, buttery smell made her wish she had a glass of white wine—and a splash for the sauce.

"So, Sarah, put me to work."

"Well…could you hand me the milk?" She picked up the whisk. He opened the quart of milk and set it next to her. She could smell the floral-alcohol scent of his cologne and thought it ruined the rich, onion smell that hung in the air.

"So…is this something your kids like you to make?" he asked.

"No. No kids." As she said those words, a pit opened up in the bottom of her gut, the rest of her body threatening to drop down through it. "My grandma's recipe." She braced herself against the counter with her left hand. "I used to make it for my dorm." She whisked in the milk in a quick, steady stream, then put down the whisk, switching back to the scraper.

"I'm sorry, I—"

"That's fine." She peeked in the stockpot again, anticipating the boil.

"It's just that, I don't know, this cooking lunch for church," Rob gestured toward the outdated kitchen. "It's so…maternal."

Sarah's face flushed and she took a hard swallow of her Diet Coke, imagining there was Jack Daniel's in it. It was as if he was testing her, as if he knew, planning to push until he got the answer he wanted. "Okay, so I do have a kid. A son."

"What? Oh." He looked confused.

"Before I said," she breathed deeply. "He's not with me. I mean he's with his dad's parents. Lives with them."

"That's too bad. I—"

"Would you mind?" Sarah nodded toward the saucepan and held the scraper toward him. "I forgot to get the pans ready."

"Sure, yeah." Rob took the scraper and began stirring, slowly, back and forth, as he'd watched her.

"Let me know if it starts to boil." Sarah was angry at herself for talking about her son to this stranger. She hated that she felt like a liar if she answered that she had no children, felt disloyal to her son. But there was no simple way to answer "yes." It was always "yes, but..." She told herself that she was going to need a new answer. That this situation would arise again and again. That this was her life now. She had no choice but to invent a way to explain it.

Sarah reached into one of her bags for two rectangular foil baking pans. She noticed the price sticker on one and scratched at it with her fingernail, removing most but leaving an opaque residue. "Damn," she whispered. She unwrapped another stick of butter, dropping it in the clean pan, before sliding it into the hot oven. She opened drawers, searching for a butter knife. "Be sure to get the bottom," she said, glancing at the sauce.

"What's that?" Rob said.

"With the scraper." She came quickly toward him and grabbed his hand. "Make sure it sweeps across the bottom surface of the pan." She raised the scraper, sighing as she showed him the coagulated sauce she had managed to remove from the saucepan's bottom, now clinging to the scraper's edge.

"Oh. Is that bad?" Rob said.

"No, here." She dug a long, wooden spoon from the drawer, handed it to Rob, and took note of the time. "Could you just pour the pasta in the pot and stir it, please?"

"Yeah, sure." He opened the boxes of rotini, poured them in the boiling water, and stirred with his arm extended, face turned away from the steam. "I um, I guess I'm a take-out kind of guy."

Sarah whisked the sauce quickly then handed the scraper back to Rob.

"It's okay, just keep going," she said. "It's hottest at the bottom so it's going to thicken-up there first." Sarah found a knife, using it to continue scratching at the sticker. "Good enough," she said, tossing the knife in the sink. It clattered more than she had intended. She opened a plastic baggie with crushed Ritz crackers and poured them into a mixing bowl. Grabbing two potholders from hooks next to the oven, she retrieved the heated pan from the oven, poured the melted butter into the second pan, and poured the butter into the bowl of cracker crumbs. She used the wrapper from the butter sticks to coat the insides of the foil pans.

She remembered once as a girl helping her grandmother prepare the pans for her birthday cake. She had helped spread pasty-white shortening inside three round pans, tasting it because it looked like icing. She gagged at the greasy film it made in her mouth. Her grandmother laughed and gave her the chocolaty batter-coated beaters to lick—always the privilege of the birthday girl. Sarah was embarrassed that she had tasted the shortening, but her grandmother told her it was something every child does, just like tasting chopped squares of bitter baking chocolate, despite the cook's insistence that they do not taste like a Hershey's bar.

Sarah wondered if her grandmother knew that she had kept all of her recipes—that she prepared what she could, alone in her apartment, picking at the food for days, tasting her grandmother's sunny kitchen and what it meant to be safe, loved.

Rob lightly tapped his toe as he stirred. Sarah feared he might start to whistle. He seemed to have music in his head to distract his thoughts. He said, "I'm sorry about asking before. I—"

"It's okay." Sarah peeked at the sauce, shook her head, and turned the heat higher. She found a spoon and stirred the butter into the crackers. Sarah felt hot and jittery, frustrated at trying to cook in a strange place, knowing how easy it would be in a familiar kitchen. Rob not knowing how to stir a béchamel angered her, too. What kind of mother doesn't teach her son how to cook for himself? She set the crackers aside and took the scraper from Rob. But then, she thought, what kind of mother would she be—would she have been—if she can't even show a man how to stir without yelling at him. "I didn't mean to get bit— ...mean about it." He laughed, knowing she had stopped herself from cursing.

"The church is all the way up there," he said, poking at the crackers with the spoon. "Swearing's allowed in a kitchen."

"I think it's a requirement," she smiled. Rob watched the rhythm of Sarah's stirring as the sauce became velvety and thick. She lowered the heat, added a few grinds from her blue plastic pepper mill and a large bag of shredded cheeses.

Above them, the bells sounded the end of the funeral service. Sarah knew the families would now be filing out of the church, driving in procession to the cemetery at the rear of the church grounds. She imagined them all standing at the graveside, pulling their coats tightly around their bodies against the October wind. The children would trace engraved names on granite headstones with chilled fingertips, sounding them out. The heels of women's shoes would puncture sparse grass, sinking into dirt. Their eyes would squint, watering from the wind, the cold, the death.

It occurred to Sarah that there must be a reason why Rob did not want to go up to the funeral service. She wondered how he knew the dead man and why he needed to hide in a kitchen, using her and her cooking as his distraction.

"So," she sighed, "I had him when I was young. My son. Well, I guess I still am young." She glanced at Rob. He seemed to purposely not make eye contact, to simply allow her to speak. "Then my boyfriend —his dad—he disappeared."

"Disappeared? You mean he just left you?" Rob's voice had a touch of anger, like a protective brother.

"Well, yes, but he actually *disappeared*. Like missing person reports and everything." Sarah turned off the heat under her sauce, moving the pan to a cold burner. "He was...not such a good guy." She half-chuckled, looked at the clock, turned off the other burner, and began searching for a colander.

"Wow, I...um."

"So, they took him." Sarah announced, her face in a lower cabinet.

"What do you mean, 'they took him'?"

"I mean, his family. They got a lawyer, filed for custody, and won." They were quiet while she was certain he was pondering the various reasons—none of them flattering—why a judge would take a child away from his mother, especially without a father. "I'm sure the family just missed him when he disappeared. Maybe thought our son would...take his place or something."

"But—"

"They said I went crazy." She sipped her Diet Coke and shook her head.

"Did you?" Rob asked simply, as if he had just asked if she had trimmed her bangs or taken out the trash.

"Only temporarily," she laughed.

"What?"

"No." She looked him hard in the face. "No, I did not go crazy. I mean, I was upset." She put a colander in the sink. "Of course, I was a little nuts for a while there, but not 'crazy,' not like officially, just... grieving, scared, lonely." She poured out the huge pot of rotini, her face lost in steam. She felt the heat softening her skin, relaxing her eyelids, her jaw. She shimmied the colander, breathed in the moist air, and tasted a piece to see that it was done. It seemed foreign, like rubber in her mouth.

"I'm sorry," he said. They heard footsteps walk into the adjacent gathering room and back out again. Someone bringing food.

"I mean, I was eighteen, I had a two-month-old baby, and my boyfriend, who I'd been trying to defend to everyone I knew—friends, family, teachers—he was just gone." Rob started to reach for her, but she stepped away instead and grabbed the buttered pans. She poured in the drained rotini, jiggled each dish to settle the pasta flat. "Look, I know this whole thing makes me seem like total trash, and I hate to even tell this story because I know how it makes people look at me."

"How?" he asked. "How do you know what people decide about you? About what happened?"

"Oh, come on. I know. I mean, I feel it myself." She stirred the sauce and poured it over the pasta, scraping it all from the saucepan, every drop. "It's like I can't believe that was me. That this is my life."

Sarah lightly stirred the sauce into the pasta, then pressed and smoothed the surfaces flat with the back of the scraper. She sprinkled a bag of shredded cheddar on top, added a layer of the cracker crumbs, and patted it all down lightly with the butter wrapper. She carried one pan to the oven, and Rob followed with the second. They slid them in, closing the oven door. "How long?" he asked.

"Just until the tops are browned. Fifteen minutes maybe." They both leaned back against the counter, staring at the oven. She wondered if the dead man had liked macaroni and cheese. "So where did you come from? For this?" Sarah asked, heading to the sink.

"San Diego," he said.

"Can you find me some towels somewhere?" She ran water into the warm stockpot, added a squirt of liquid soap. Rob opened a couple of drawers until he found some folded dish towels. "San Diego, huh? So, you must hate coming here to the cold weather."

"No, not really. I miss the seasons," he said. He picked-up the empty baggies and wrappers and threw them away.

Sarah washed the pot, then poured its soapy water into the sauce pot in the sink. She breathed deeply to try to stretch the tension from her shoulders, wondering if her son liked to play in the bubbles in his bath, if they showed him her picture—"see the crazy lady?" She wondered if he watched his grandmother cook, if he was afraid of the blender, if he was ever given macaroni and cheese from the oven or just from a box.

"Here, let me dry." He took the rinsed pot from her. "And I miss Ohio food. My God, I can't imagine how long it's been since I've had homemade macaroni and cheese."

Footsteps echoed in the hallway and a woman came into the kitchen.

"Hello!" she sang out. "You must be Sarah." She set a foil-covered casserole on the counter then hung her coat. "Smells yummy. And you are?" She reached for Rob's hand.

"Rob." He shook her hand. "Robert Sadowski. I'm just uh, just here too early." He gestured towards his black suit. The woman turned and reached for paper plates and plastic silverware in an upper cabinet.

"Oh, I see. I'm sorry for your loss. I'm Gayle. Are you related to Claude and Margaret?" She asked and immediately walked out of the kitchen to the gathering room, requiring him to follow in order to answer her. Rob glanced at Sarah, chuckling, then grabbed a stack of cups from the open cupboard and followed Gayle.

"Yes, my aunt and uncle," Rob said, handing Gayle the cups. An old woman shuffled in with a plate of oatmeal cookies. She set them on the table, smiled, and left.

"Thanks so much, Leona!" Gayle called after her. "Robert, you can start the coffee. You do know how to make coffee, yes?" Gayle raised the metal blind and opened the cafeteria-style counter between the kitchen and gathering room. The metal clattered and brightness spilled into that side of the kitchen.

Sarah listened to their voices and the footsteps of people streaming in and out, bringing food. She remembered the only funeral she had ever been to, just a few weeks before. Upstairs in the church, she had knelt on the brown vinyl kneeler along the oak pew. She had stared at the terrazzo floor and smelled the incense wafting from the burner swaying in the priest's hands.

"Father's cooking something," a child had whispered behind her.

Sarah remembered staring all around the church, memorizing the stained-glass stories, studying the plaster-carved angels, and counting the steps to the altar, to the wedding rail, to the podium. She had done everything to avoid thinking about the fact that they were there to mourn her grandmother, the one person who had said "congratulations" when her son had been born, who had brought pumpkin bread and held the sleeping infant while Sarah dozed in the dim afternoon of her basement apartment, the one person who said, "I'm so sorry" when her boyfriend was gone.

"Oh, here, let me," Gayle said near the coffee urn. Sarah turned to see Gayle take the oversized paper filter out of Rob's hands and nudge him out of the way with a wag of her hips. "You go find more napkins, please."

Rob looked at Sarah and mouthed *please*, nodding in mock surprise, as he started to look for more napkins. Sarah took her pans from the oven and carried one out to the room. A pair of ladies had arrived and were removing foil from their dishes on the table, revealing what they had to share.

"Afternoon," Sarah said, setting her dish on a trivet. She was pleased with the brownness of the crusty surface, the cheese sauce bubbling at the crevices and edges. The ladies smiled their approval and left.

Sarah looked at the table filled with food that had appeared when she was in the kitchen. There was green bean casserole with mushrooms, whipped potatoes, and biscuit-topped chicken pot pie. Creamy carrot-raisin salad, and a fruit salad of pineapple, red grapes, chopped Granny Smiths, and poppyseed dressing. Lemon squares dusted with powdered sugar and chocolaty Texas sheet cake.

"Hello, dear," a woman said, placing a plastic platter with zucchini bread slices fanned-out, and a small plastic bowl of cream cheese spread flecked with chopped walnuts.

"Thank you," Sarah whispered. She remembered pausing at the table, after her grandmother's burial, a serving spoon in her hand, and realizing that no one in her own family had made the food spread before her. Like the cobbler's elves, these women had lovingly worked in separate kitchens, delivered their wares, and had gone on with their days. She felt this must be what women had done for each other's families for centuries—this system that she had never known about because she had never needed it before, never been part of it before, a system devised especially for death.

But there is no meal arranged to mourn the loss of someone still alive.

Sarah returned to the kitchen. Rob was leaning against the counter. She rinsed the sink quietly, dried the faucet, the rim. Dressy-shoed footsteps and low voices soon swelled in the corridor and drifted into the gathering room. "Well, I guess I'll need to be getting out there, huh?" Rob said.

"Yeah, I guess so." Sarah sensed his gentle dread. She thought he did not seem particularly saddened by the death. He seemed more afraid to face the grievers. "Hey, thanks for your help," she said. "This is my first time doing this and, well it's a little...strange." She had finished drying the dishes. People now filled the adjacent room.

"Nice meeting you." He shook her hand softly. "And...good luck." He smiled quickly, warmly, and left.

Sarah kept her back to the gathering room. The voices were louder than she had imagined they would be. Some whispered, some exclaimed joy at seeing those they had not seen in a long time. Some, surprisingly, laughed—likely the young. She tried to listen for Rob's voice, wondering if maybe he had left altogether. She hoped all of the casseroles stayed properly hot for them, and the fruits nicely chilled. She hoped the coffee urn stayed full, stayed fresh, and that everything felt a little good going down.

"Well," Gayle said, returning to the kitchen. "I'll be back in an hour or so to start cleaning up out there." She put on her coat. Sarah nodded. "Another gal will come too. You can just finish up here then be on your way. Unless you want to stay. It's up to you." She smiled, then breezed out of the kitchen, returning it to stillness.

"Damn. Nutmeg," Sarah said, spotting the forgotten tin on the counter.

She was left again with the gatherers' voices. She wondered if they were all telling stories about the dead man. Explaining how they knew him, were affected by him, laying claim to their grief. Or were they simply speaking to fill the air? Chatting about their new boss, last week's windstorm, the impressive number of squashes their garden had yielded, anything else they could say to avoid acknowledging the death. Sarah thought they might be able to set it aside, to distract themselves, but eventually their grief would rise in their bellies, and would pulse through their throats with the steady, wheezing throb of a car engine resisting winter. Someday—despite their attempts to ignore it, despite hurriedly arranging the rest of life in front of it—someday they would realize that their grief could break them down.

Sarah listened to the rumble of their voices and suddenly needed to leave, to get them out of her head. She put away the saucepan and pot. She put away the colander and the mixing bowl, the wooden spoon and the whisk. She put everything away.

✧ ✧ ✧

Ohio born and raised, **Kerry Trautman** is a founder of Toledopoet.com and the "Toledo Poetry Museum" page on Facebook. Her poetry and short fiction have appeared in various journals, including Midwestern Gothic, Alimentum, Hawaii Pacific Review, The Fourth River, and Slippery Elm; as well as in anthologies such as, Delirious: A Poetic Celebration of Prince (NightBallet Press 2016), Mourning Sickness

(Omniarts 2008), Nine Lives Later: A Dead Cat Anthology (Barely Salvageable Press 2017), and, of course, Not Quite as You Were Told (Dandelion Revolution Press 2020). Her poetry books are Things That Come in Boxes (King Craft Press 2012), To Have Hoped (Finishing Line Press 2015), Artifacts (NightBallet Press 2017), and To be Nonchalantly Alive (Kelsay Books 2020.)

14

WALKING IN HER SHOES

New York, Spring 1979

Mamma let's read now! When are we going to California?" I asked, holding the library books about California. We were going to leave our house in Queens, New York and join Pappa. He was finding a new house for us where we could go to the beach and swim in the Pacific Ocean all year.

"When you finish first grade in a few weeks, we will go. In the meantime, Divya, let's learn all we can. Before I came to the United States and after I got married to your Pappa, I watched movies and read books to improve my English. If I keep staring at these books with the sun and beaches, I'm going to get a tan myself," she giggled. I laughed with her, but I didn't understand. Mamma said Indian women didn't need to become tan like the blonde women on "Charlie's Angels."

Mamma and I did a lot of reading and coloring when we were home together; Pappa took a bus to work in New York City in the morning and came home late. Sometimes, I played with Michelle across the street after school; sometimes we rode our bikes around the block or listened to her older sister's "Grease" album.

"Did we get any postcards today? Pappa said he would send me a postcard." I started to run to the front door to see the mailbox. Mamma stepped in front of me.

"No, Divya *béta*, I haven't seen anything. He will." She guided me back to the living room towards the library books. "He said he'll write since it's too expensive to call long distance. Your Pappa is such a pioneer. Remember we saw that book about the pioneers? They had those covered wagons and log cabins?" I nodded. "So, he's staying with Dilip Uncle's cousin in Los Angeles. He knows a man in California who is going to help him start his own accounting business. Once he's settled, he'll come get us."

I thought of Pappa's face when he would walk in the house. His big smile would push his cheeks up so much that his dark eyes would disappear. He always lifted and spun me around and called me "Chiku." He would come back soon.

Weeks passed and school ended, but we didn't hear from him. Mamma was on the phone calling everyone in her blue address book.

"Dilip *Bhai*, but it was a wrong number. Yes, he said he was staying with your cousin in California." She twirled the cord of the phone around her fingers, and kept her voice friendly. "Are you sure you don't have any relatives there? Maybe someone else? Yes, please call me back."

Mamma hung up the yellow phone on the kitchen wall and flopped into a seat at the small wooden table. Four chairs with bright yellow flowers surrounded it with a white plastic tablecloth. Mamma opened one of the library books. She wasn't reading, just turning pages. Her face was heavy with sadness, eyes glassy and mouth down-turned. I climbed on one of the yellow chairs to hug her. She smiled.

"Mamma, did you check the mail today? Maybe we got a postcard?" I suggested. That would definitely make her happy again. I still wanted to see what a postcard looked like!

"Good idea, baby. Let's go check?" she said. We checked the small black mailbox outside the front door. It was like magic when Mamma pulled out letters and magazines.

"Yes, there's a letter from him!" she said. I could read "Mrs. Jyothi Ashok Joshi" and our address written in square letters. There was nothing else on the front of the envelope; I wished he had written "Divya" or "Chiku."

We scurried back to the living room and Mamma sat on our orange sofa, sunlight streaming through the large front windows. While she was reading, her eyes filled with tears and she collapsed sobbing. She buried her head in her hands and her shoulders shook as she cried. I could see the curly letters of Gujarati on the page and I wanted to ask her what he said.

"Mamma don't cry. It's going to be okay," I said softly. I stroked her head like she always did mine when I was sad. "Can I give you a kissy?"

She gazed at me with red eyes and broke into a smile. "Yes, *béta*, give me a kissy. And I'll give you two kissies back."

I threw my arms around her neck and felt her wet tears on my cheek. I could help her feel better. I would not talk about California anymore.

Later that night, I was in my room practicing reading words to my dolls when I overheard Mamma on the phone with her sister, Anji Masi. She switched between crying and shouting into the phone in Gujarati and English. I crept from my bedroom to the hallway corner, where I could see her, but still stay hidden.

"Ashok wants a divorce! A girlfriend? What is wrong with him! Why did he even bother coming back to India to get married? It's my fault—I should not have gotten married quickly. I was only 22 and I said yes because our grandfathers were friends. Remember, he said he needed to return for work in two weeks. *Arré, arré*, what a fool I was." She shook her head.

"Now we know why he had to go back! I'm telling you, my daughter is not going to have an arranged marriage. Why should I even give Ashok a divorce? What kind of man leaves his wife and small child alone in this country? He wants to sell the house because it's in his name," she exclaimed. Then her brows furrowed as she leaned forward on the kitchen table. "What? No, I'm not going to go back to India. I can't. I'm too ashamed." She wept into the phone, covering her face.

I retreated back to my bedroom and closed the door. I looked in the dressing table mirror and tried to say the word "divorce." *Dee-voor..ss.* I didn't know what it meant, but it seemed so bad. He wanted it, but how was he going to take it? I scanned my bedroom, wondering what it looked like and where it was.

I peered at my reflection. People always said I was a "carbon copy" of my father with my sharp nose, yet I had Mamma's smile with a dimple. Mamma had cut my straight black hair short, even though I wanted long hair like hers. She said short was better, but I thought I looked like a boy. They only know I'm a girl because of my little gold earrings and the short ponytail spouting on top of my head like a fountain. I could hear Mamma still shouting, so I sang "Grease" songs softly to myself.

I would not talk about Pappa anymore.

One day, Mamma and I were eating kheer, a special sweet rice pudding, for dinner and she made an announcement. "I've got big news, Divya. Mamma got a job! I'm going to be working at a bank!"

"At the desk with the lollipops?" My eyes widened. Mamma laughed.

"Yes, as a teller. And… we're going to move to a new apartment. Dilip Uncle helped me find an apartment and this house is being sold. We're going to be pioneers!"

"Do we need a covered wagon?" I asked.

She shook her head. "No, a moving truck will come to take all our things next week. We will have to pack up whatever we can."

"Can I bring my library books? Is Pappa going to meet us there? How will he know where to find us?" I asked.

Mamma took a deep breath and explained Pappa would live in a different house. She twisted her mouth to the side as she said she didn't know when we'd see him again. But how would Pappa find us if we were not in this house? They told me if I ever got lost, I should stay in one place. I gazed into her deep brown eyes and swallowed my questions. I didn't want her to cry.

"Don't worry. You'll be at your same school, and you'll see your friends again in September!" she said with a smile. I nodded.

On moving day, the men packed all the furniture and boxes into the truck. I tried to see the inside of the truck, but everyone told me to stay back. Raj Masa waited at the apartment and Anji Masi came to drive us in her Ford station wagon. I sat in the backseat reading my books. Mamma placed more bags next to me and made me sit on some of them. She was wearing a maroon cotton kurta over her jeans with blue sneakers. Her long hair was braided, but loose strands had fallen on her face.

"Let me do one last check," Anji Masi said as she walked back into the house. She returned and stood on the white front stoop, holding a pair of brown wooden heels in the air. "Jyothi, what are these? Are they yours? Do you want them?" She scrunched her nose.

Mamma raised her head from the car and pushed her hair back to see better.

"Those? Ashok gave those to me when I came to the US in '72," she called. Mamma left the car door open as she walked up the path to get the shoes.

"You know, first, he told me to stop wearing saris and to start wearing skirts like American girls. I told him I am a married woman now, not a silly schoolgirl wearing small skirts. Then he got me these ugly shoes. He said it's in fashion. Platform shoes. I told him I'm going to break my ankle walking in those wooden things with a stroller in the city," she said, pointing her finger in the air as if she was scolding him.

"You know, he was always telling me to change. Loosen my hair from the bun, fine. Then he told me to cut my hair and I refused. People know us for our long hair, Anji." She pulled her long braid forward. "He said eat meat... drink wine... you have to fit into this culture... Enough! Give me those shoes!"

Mamma snatched the shoes out of Anji Masi's hands and stormed across the grass towards the living room windows. I heard a crash of glass and I jumped. Mamma was using the wooden shoes to smash the windows! When the glass had shattered into a big enough hole, she threw the shoe inside. She went to the next window and used the other shoe to break the glass. I could hear her muttering but didn't know what she said.

Anji Masi screamed, "Jyothi! What are you doing? Are you crazy? *Tu paagal che?*"

"No, I'm not! I'm just giving him back his shoes! Giving back his house!" Mamma turned and walked towards the car. She brushed her hands together and dusted dirt from her maroon top.

"Let's go, Anji. We are done." More hair had fallen out of her braid, so she pushed her hair back off her face. She walked just like Charlie's Angels back to the car.

New Jersey, Fall 1989

"Divya, there are some garage sales we can go see today," Mamma called to me from downstairs, as she was reading the newspaper. "I need to find a small shovel for the garden."

Ever since we moved into our New Jersey house five years ago, Mamma and I became regular garage sale and outlet shoppers. Friends offered to sell their house to us when they moved, and Mamma had jumped at the chance to leave our Queens apartment. It worked out even better when she transferred to the local bank branch as a supervisor.

The garage sales gave Mamma a chance to practice driving around town since we bought a new Chevy. At the time, I was loving Pet Shop Boys' "Suburbia" and Madness singing about "Our House;" it felt exciting to be in the 'burbs and out of the city. But once we moved, the silence was so loud that it kept us awake at night. I missed the yaps of the neighborhood dogs after firetrucks whizzed by. Nevertheless, we got used to it. It had been tougher getting used to the new middle school; they teased me about my New York accent until I lost it by high school.

Mamma said she was happy we would finally be "settled," but truly, she was more excited to have space to decorate. It was an older split-level house; the rooms needed paint and the backyard needed love. The "Reader's Digest Guide to House Repairs" was her handbook to fix things before she called a handyman. She hand painted the name "Trivedi" on the mailbox, since we changed our names after the divorce. I remember I practiced writing Divya Trivedi without the Joshi in second grade,until it felt right.

When I came downstairs from my bedroom, I knew she would be in the living room, sitting on our olive green chenille sofa with the Sunday *New York Times* and a cup of chai with Nabisco Social Tea biscuits on the coffee table. Today, she wore her purple flowered kurta with yellow and red pyjamas, her legs tucked under her and her house slippers on the floor. She didn't care if the tunic prints clashed with the flowy pants, as long as she was comfortable. Mamma's clothes always seemed bigger than her slim frame. Her hair was in her usual braid down her back and there was a shadow of yesterday's eyeliner on her face. She barely noticed me, dressed in my torn jeans and tie-dyed Depeche Mode shirt. I refused to allow her to cut my hair anymore, so I let my hair freely hang below my shoulders.

"Hey Mamma, I wrote this for my creative writing class. Can you read it for me?" I asked.

"Of course, Divya *béta*. You know I love reading your work. Push your hair back so I can see your face." She smiled with the dimples gracing her cheeks, and accepted the typed page I presented to her. She read quietly with little expression on her face as I stood, anxiously awaiting. When she was done, she flipped the paper over to see if there would be more.

"Hmph," she said, inspecting the blank back page.

"What is it?" I asked. I couldn't tell what she was thinking.

Mamma scrunched her nose. "It's a horrible poem, Divya. All those dirty references."

"What?" I exclaimed. "What do you mean? This is a poem about female empowerment! Reclaiming our bodies and our lives!"

"Divya, tell me. Is this what they teach you in high school now? What happened to Robert Frost and all those classic poems? *'The woods are lovely, dark and deep... but I have promises to keep... and miles to go before I sleep?'* You shouldn't write like this," she said, twisting her mouth to the side, as usual. "Poetry should be clean and pretty. See, we cut our teeth on nursery rhymes and they're light... and refreshing!" she chirped.

"Are you kidding me? I'm not going to write nursery rhymes. I'm sixteen years old," I said, as I took a hair tie from my wrist to pull my hair into a ponytail.

"No, I'm not saying that. Poetry should slide down your throat like cool water. It should be part of your body. Think of all the great *shayaris*, our Hindi and Urdu poems. They lift your spirit. Touch your soul. Reading a poem like this is like eating a spicy samosa and trying to soothe your mouth with a fizzy Coca-Cola instead of water. Your thirst is still there."

She glared at me as if it should be obvious. I stared back at her. What does a fried pastry stuffed with potatoes have to do with my poem? A stray strand of black hair hung on her face. I waited. She pushed the hair over her ear and leaned in to continue.

"*Arré*, imagine you are at a party, eating a samosa and you eat a green chili by accident. Now your tongue is all spicy, right? It's a party and all you have is Coca-Cola. Of course, you drink it, but now the fizz tingles and sticks in the back of your throat. It is painful! All you can do is cough. Now your mouth is sweet, but your thirst is still there and your throat hurts. No, thank you. You need a sunny, cool glass of ice water. Now, Divya *béta*, do work on something more cheerful," she said as she handed me the paper.

"And, go get me a glass of water." She leaned to pick up her newspapers from the table, plucked the coupon sections and began to thumb through the pages.

"Ok. Fine!" I was fuming as I went to the kitchen. I slammed a cabinet or two for effect so she would know I was mad. This is the last time I will ever share my work with her. Even if I win the Pulitzer... no... the Nobel Prize, she will have to wait and buy my books herself. I'm not going to let her see any more of my work. What's the point? Jyothi Trivedi was not ready to hear anything other than what she wanted to hear.

I returned with a glass of water, which she accepted graciously, even as I offered it silently.

"By the way, here's the Sunday magazine for you. Your poetry is good, but remember, we cannot just write stories all day. You know, we are Indian. We are not from this country and must be practical. *Béta*, your science grades are good. You could go to medical school like Ravi. Remember how he cried when he got ninety-eight percent on a test? What a son Anji has!" she beamed.

I rolled my eyes, thinking of my cousin Ravi. He was not as goody-goody as she thought he was. I saw him drunk and puking at football games when I visited him in college last year. But I can't be mad at him. It's not his fault our mothers only talk about this stuff.

"Okay, fine," I said as I stomped back to my room with my paper and magazine section.

Once in the privacy of my room, I briefly examined my poem and tucked it into my folders. Of course, she would say I need to be practical, since that's what was expected of her, demanded really. She had no choice to follow her heart. It was all survival. Ravi suggested once that since I liked to read and write, I should look into pre-law programs. Indians needed to be doctors, lawyers, engineers, or maybe all three. The more degrees one had after their name, the better bragging rights for their parents.

I pressed "Play" on my double cassette player that sat on my dresser. With the volume of my Depeche Mode's album on high, I flopped onto my bed, tired of thinking about life and my future. Craving samosas and a Coke.

New Jersey, Spring 1999

"I'm happy you're here! Let's eat dinner and you can tell me all about Chicago!" Mamma said, pulling into the driveway as we returned from the airport. It felt so good to see colorful azaleas and peonies in bloom in the front yard. The neighborhood seemed to sparkle more every spring.

I kicked off my black slingback pumps next to Mom's kitten-heeled beige sandals by the door. I ran to my bedroom to change into my old Rutgers sweats, anxious to be free of my Ann Taylor skirts. I took a wistful glance around my childhood bedroom. It always seemed to look smaller than I remembered. A few stuffed animals sat on my pink and white comforter, while a box of CDs and cassettes was shoved in a corner. My English lit, women's studies and law books fought for space on the bookshelves; a few casualties were stacked on the floor, beside my old journals.

When I came down, Mamma was prepping dinner, still dressed in her work clothes—a dusty rose sweater with a lavender scarf over black slacks. Her bangles clinked as she moved in the kitchen. She had a new haircut, still long but with layers framing her face. She looked ageless with her naturally petite figure; people were always surprised to learn she was the mother of a grown daughter and I could see why.

I smelled my favorite dish as I walked into the kitchen—her special Indianized pasta with sautéed onions, peppers, and a good dose of spiced garlic oil and tandoori masala in tomato sauce. It combined the best of all comfort foods into one dish. The blue and white Corningware plates sitting on top of a new white vinyl tablecloth felt familiar, as if nothing had changed. I poured Diet Coke into a couple of glasses with ice and let the fizz tickle my nose before taking a quick sip. I jumped into my seat, ready to eat.

"This is so good. I missed this," I said as I reached for more parmesan cheese for the pasta, while she added extra red pepper flakes to her plate. In between bites, I told her about my work with the women's legal center, writing articles for their websites, and how different the social scene was in Chicago. Mamma followed along intently, interrupting to ask clarifying questions.

""Who is that? Was he the one who went to NYU? Have I met them before? Why did they move to Chicago?"

"Mamma, you should've been a lawyer with all these questions!" I laughed.

"No, no, one lawyer in the family is good enough. But I have some surprise news for you." I paused from eating to look at her before she continued. "I'm going to school! The bank is offering programming courses to train on their new financial systems."

"Mamma, that's good for you!" I said.

"Once I get this certificate, I can be a programmer and maybe one day, a manager. It starts in a few weeks, so I'm a little nervous."

"Oh please! You've been there for years, you could be teaching them! We should celebrate."

"Well, it's Mother's Day tomorrow so we will be celebrating." Mamma continued to give me updates on friends and family, including Suneel Uncle whose new friend Jorge she met recently.

"What about you, Mamma? When will you start meeting someone?"

Over the years, friends and family had tried to introduce her to men. At first, she refused, saying, "I already have a child, I don't need another." But, these days, she admitted she was open to introductions for the sake of companionship.

"Okay, fine. I was going to tell you that too."

"Wow, another surprise tonight! What is it?"

"Well, his name is Dev and he's Anji's neighbor. It's not so serious," she said, sipping her soda. "We just talk on the phone and go out for coffee or dinner sometimes." She added more pepper to her pasta to avoid looking at me.

"Okay... tell me more about him." I slowly took a bite of my pasta, looking at her.

"We met last year... he's a software engineer. He's very busy working on all these projects. You know, they're expecting big computer crashes all over the world in 2000? It's not good." She shook her head at the bleak outlook.

"Mamma..."

"Yah, we started meeting over the summer. It's good. Since you're staying a few days, you can meet him before you leave. And, by the way, Anji Masi and Raj Masa are coming to meet you tonight. They're bringing dessert."

"Oh? Tonight?" I wiped my mouth with my napkin. "I should go change before they come! I'm a mess."

"No rush. They're coming at 8:30. You can have some more pasta," she said, more of a directive than a question as she scooped extra onto my plate. "See, you've got some color in your face already. You needed good food."

When we finished, Mamma nudged me out of the way as I tried to do the dishes. "I'll do this. When you go upstairs, look for your mail on my desk. I think it's your tax refund."

Walking into my mother's light blue bedroom, I noticed it was organized exactly as it had been for years. A floral comforter lay on her bed, accented with a few Indian embroidered pillows. On her oak dressing table, her perfume collections were displayed on a mirrored tray while her comb, compact, lipstick, and eyeliner sat on another tray. In the corner of the room stood her small oak desk where she filed important papers and bills. I wasn't allowed to touch her tables when I was younger, so consequently that corner seemed to glow with importance. The table was neatly ordered, but I didn't see any envelopes for me, just her notebooks and ledgers. Perhaps she had put the mail in the drawers.

When I opened the top drawer, I noticed a large brown envelope that looked quite worn with her name and our old Queens apartment address. A red string tied the envelope closed and I unwound it to peer inside. There were about fifteen to twenty envelopes addressed to my mother, some still sealed. I looked inside one of the opened envelopes and saw a handwritten check. It was to Jyothi Trivedi from the account of Ashok Joshi. The memo line said, "For Chiku."

I had never seen his handwriting before. Mamma had removed all his photographs from the albums, so he was always a Shadow Man to me. His signatures proved that he was real. It was very angular and tight, hard to discern his name. The checks had a New York street address. Is he still there?

I pulled another envelope and another, finding checks tucked inside each. There was one check with a Florida address in 1985. I held a sealed envelope to the light and could see the outline of a check. In addition to the envelopes, there were dozens of bank statements for an account in my mother's name.

"Mamma, what is this?" I hollered. "Mamma!"

"What is it?" she called as she came up the stairs to the bedroom, wiping her hands on a kitchen towel.

"What are all these checks? They're uncashed." I held the checks in front of her and dropped the rest of the envelopes and bank statements on the bed.

"Oh no, why did you go in there? I told you to get your mail only. It's right there on top. Can't you see?" Mamma plucked the big envelope out of my hands and handed me my letters, which were on the dressing table.

"Are these child support checks? They're all dated twenty years ago. Why didn't you cash them? You needed the money." I thought of all the times she struggled to make her paycheck last. She expertly negotiated with bill collectors, promising to pay off debts in small increments, and would drop in a story about being a single mother to get an extension.

"When we got divorced, the lawyers said he needed to pay child support. He didn't want the visitation. But, go ahead and count them. That's all he sent," she said, crossing her arms and lifting her chin.

I looked through the stack and checked the dates. "That's it? But why did he stop sending?" I asked.

"Who knows, *béta*. But I don't care. It's fine with me. At the end, you know everything you have is from your mother's hard work. No donations. I can show you another envelope with checks my parents sent me from India. I didn't cash theirs either. Instead, I started sending them money once my jobs started doing well." Mamma pushed a lock of hair behind her ear, looking at me.

"You got all those scholarships, my sweet smart girl." She reached out to pinch my cheek and puckered her lips. I shirked away, shaking my head at her.

"You could have at least put this in a bank account. Collected interest! Are these expired?" She stayed calm as I grew more frustrated.

"Yes, I could have. But I didn't. It is money and there's value to *you* when you cash it. The value to *me* is when I have it in my hand. This is how I was raised—a woman has to have means to her own security," she explained. "Haven't I lived my life without obligations to anyone? I've enjoyed my freedom and look at you now. It breaks my heart to let you go away, but you're like my kite. I have put you in the air and let you fly free. You're still tied to me and you know the way home. For me, I put my past behind and cut the ties. We're flying now, aren't we?"

She put her hand on my shoulder and I tried to comprehend her perspective. It all seemed like the years and emotions blurred together.

"Honestly, I'm surprised you found these checks. I thought you'd see this envelope first." She reached into the drawer and pulled out another full envelope with my name in red marker.

"Look inside," she said with a gleam in her eyes.

I tilted the envelope to pull the contents. There were birthday cards and Mother's Day cards that I had given her over the years. My childish handwriting looked full of love and hopefulness. A folded piece of typed paper was in the midst, which I opened.

"My poem? You kept this?"

"Of course, my darling daughter wrote this! It was beautiful! I had to keep it since I read it so many times," she smiled.

"You told me you hated it."

"Oh please, I never said that! I have saved everything you gave me." She gazed at me warmly. Gently taking the yellow envelope and with her arm around me, she led me to her dressing table.

"Come, we have a lot to look forward to now. *Chaalo*, let's go... Anji Masi will be here soon. Can you help me fix my eyeliner?" she said, picking up the black tube from the mirror tray.

I put the envelopes back on her desk and looked at her critically for a moment before speaking. What could I say at this point? She had her reasons and who was I to say otherwise? She was just a few years older than I was now. Maybe I would've done the same in her shoes.

"Of course. But you need better lipstick. I've got a new one you can try," I said cheerfully. "Let me get it!"

"Oh? I'll try it. It'll be a nice change," she said, leaning into the mirror to fix her hair in her reflection.

As I watched her, I thought, this is how you fly free.

✧ ✧ ✧

Ashini J. Desai is a co-founder of Dandelion Revolution Press and balances creative writing with family and a technology management career. Her poems, essays and short stories have been published in various literary journals and anthologies, and she has written columns for South Asian-American websites. Her short story was published in "Not Quite As You Were Told" anthology. Her personal website with selected poems is ashinipoetry.blogspot.com and on Instagram as @AshiniWrites.

15

THE PUPPETEER

T hank you all for being here," I said with my facial muscles fixed on what I remembered to be a smile. I had practiced the movement in the mirror so often, the muscle memory had become second nature, though I'll never get used to seeing the fleshy hag with tacky red lipstick reflected back at me.

"This is a matter of grave concern for all of us," I asserted. Pressing my lips, I lowered my brow and flared my nostrils. The best puppeteers are able to express emotion where there is none.

"My administration is taking every step to deal with this crisis. My highest priority is the safety of my constituents," I continued, as a fresh, meaty scent betrayed my nostrils. My eyes flashed into the crowd, darkened by night, beyond the pre-selected reporters and their blaring lights. Time slowed as I scanned for the origin of the scent, before blinking my gaze back to the cameras.

"Clean drinking water is a right, which is why an independent investigation has been launched," I said, sternly raising my brow, lips briefly curling. Saliva began to pool under my tongue. I paused my speaking cadence to gulp down the hot liquid. Unable to see what I could smell, my eyes slid across the view of reporters.

"The Saintsville water supply will return to the reservoir and justice will be served. I will see to it myself." I pushed my lips slightly forward and tilted my neck up fifteen degrees. Every subtle movement, part of the show; deep in the pit of my grumbling stomach, I could feel the act falling apart.

"As soon as my administration discovers who is responsi—" the word caught in my throat and I tried my hardest not to cough. Sticky phlegm coated my vocal chords and sprayed into my lungs with every gasp. Without having to say a word, Sylvia, my rock, had a bottle of water with the top unscrewed in her out-stretched arm. Taking it, I drank a timid sip, just big enough to wash out my throat, before I handed the bottle back to Sylvia with a harrumph.

"Those responsible will be held accountable," I asserted, trying to regain my composure. Sylvia stepped up next to me to speak into the microphone.

"We have time for just a few questions," she said, and half a dozen hands went up.

"Yes," I said, as I pointed to a recognizable blonde. The crowd beyond began to disperse in waves, their shadowy figures replaced by the shimmering lights reflected off the still reservoir. Sparse streetlights revealed the government plaza to be especially busy, with groups of tourists still departing. Their echoes of laughter felt more like taunts. My nostrils burned with the scent of fresh meat, wafting ever closer in the warm breeze.

"Thank you, Governor Valentine. Ma'am, what is the timeline of the independent investigation?"

I pushed up my cheeks and squinted as I curved the edges of my mouth, head tilted twenty degrees right. "Undetermined, at this point. When I know, you will know." Re-centering my head, I promptly nodded, and the blonde sat down as others raised their hands.

"Yes," I said to the next shiny face, plastered with gratitude.

"Governor Valentine, what is your response to the allegation of negligence from your office?"

Pushing my cheeks up even higher, I said, "I don't traffic rumors, nor do I grant them credence."

"Yes, ma'am," he responded, sitting down.

Sylvia spoke into the microphone. "That's all the time we have for questions tonight," she said. All the reporters stood up as camera operators began packing equipment. My lingering smile sat comfortably across my face. As the camera lights clicked off, the crowd became easier to see.

The government plaza had a few stragglers moseying away, aside from a group behind the press box—probably waiting for a glimpse of my greatness. Their forms coming into focus, I observed closer, and sucked in deeply through my nose.

"Who gave the order to switch the Saintsville water supply from the reservoir to the river?" shouted a tiny voice near the press box. I looked down to see a stick figure of a girl, holding out a sideways smartphone, filming me. My easy smile remained unchanged. She stepped closer to my podium, past the press box. A large man from security stepped forward but I waved him down with a sideways scrunch of my eyebrow, and he went at-ease.

"When they made the order, they knew the industrial waste would poison the citizens," she continued. Her scent, like chlorinated cigarette smoke, sickened me. With unkempt locks of black hair, she looked to be sixteen years old, yet her impurities were palpable. It was rare for someone so young to be so... tainted. Behind her, a fresher, more alluring scent lingered, somewhere in the bustling crowd. "How do you not know who made that decision?"

My smile grew full and I clasped my hands. "I know you don't understand how this works yet, but there is a level of decorum required to have a civil conversation and you're being very rude."

Like a sparkling gem, the creature my nose had been fawning over caught my eye. My head snapped ten degrees to the left and my eyes focused into the crowd, easier now without the bright lights in my face. Wetness filled my mouth as I spotted the small, pure child, who was watching a street performance. Then, as if reading my mind, he turned and looked right at me from across the plaza. The wannabe reporter kept whining at me, but her words didn't register and sounded like chirping, as my brain fell into a primal pattern, my thoughts quickening. The young boy appeared unattended. It felt like an act of God. The planets aligning. My stomach growling.

"That's all the time we have for questions," Sylvia said into the microphone. "Let's go." She placed her hand on my shoulder, as if to usher me away.

"No," I said, looking into her blue eyes. "I'd like to go for a walk." She nodded, and I turned back to the girl in front of my podium.

"Please refer to my statement if you have any more questions about the situation." Her little face squirmed into an amusing scowl. I could feel her hatred pour into me and it felt good. I walked past her, Sylvia at my side and two security guards following.

Descending the stone stairs of the Capitol building, I scanned the sparse crowd that remained. The awe-stricken would soon ambush me for their chance to gaze upon real power. I knew exactly how to use that energy. My prize—my prey—was waiting for me.

Another set of concrete stairs led me to the main plaza, a large square, lined with red buildings in the shape of a U, the Capitol being at the center. The far end formed a terrace over the bay, where pedestrians mingled. As I advanced into the darkness, the sweet, delicious scents flooding my nose confirmed I was growing nearer.

In front of the terrace, about two dozen people stood around a street performer, including the boy. No one looked my way as I approached. That struck me as odd, but I used it to my advantage, closing my eyes.

I stilled my body, my heartbeat slowing. My consciousness vibrated through my skull, rising above my head. In astral mode, I moved left through the crowd, towards the child. I burrowed myself into his head, fitting comfortably inside. I disabled his motor functions and returned to my body.

The child's gaze remained still, facing the performer, his jaw hanging open, eyes glazed over. The rest of the crowd still had yet to notice me, too fixated on the show.

I looked to see what kind of act was keeping their attention. It was a puppeteer. Using strings, the gray-haired man manipulated a wooden puppet at his feet, among other props. Then I realized the puppet looked just like me, down to my watch.

In a miniature pantsuit and blonde wig, the puppet over-indulged in cake, smearing frosting on its face. Then it saw the polls on a television prop and began crying into the cake. It heaved sobs and shoved more cake into its mouth. The whole audience erupted in laughter.

It wasn't my depiction that got to me, nor the mindless scene that lit a fury in my empty belly.

It was the fact that he was so good at it.

The wooden doll was surprisingly expressive, with moving parts on the face to show exaggerated emotions. It wiped the mess off its face and then looked in the mirror and started crying again.

"Danger is in every glass of water, thanks to you!" The foul girl had followed from the Capitol building and continued shouting behind me. "And you can't even answer for your actions."

Eyes in the crowd began turning to me. The gray man's face lit up and the puppet gasped, pointed and waved. The young boy continued looking forward with his jaw hanging. The puppet gestured to the girl, drank a fake glass of water, then feigned collapsing. Everyone in the crowd continued laughing—except the child, who remained motionless.

The government plaza and the whole upper West side still drank from the reservoir—this well-dressed audience was unaffected and uninterested in the water quality past the train tracks.

I let out a hearty chuckle loud enough for everyone to hear. Even Sylvia and my guards started laughing. I covered my mouth and leaned forward as the fits consumed me. I leaned back with an exasperated sigh and smiled cheerfully to the crowd. Raising my hand into the air toward the puppeteer, I declared:

"Magnificent! A true artist!"

No one plays me better than me.

The man and his puppet bowed. I bowed in return, first to him and then to the audience. Everyone applauded.

I felt the boy snap out of my mental grasp and saw him run past me.

"Jilly, I want to go home," I heard him cry behind my back. I spun around to see him pulling on the pant leg of the wannabe reporter, her phone pointed at me—the two of them encircled by Sylvia and my security.

"Stop it, Caleb, I'm almost done," she murmured at him.

"I don't feel good, I want to go home," he said.

I placed my hand on the small child's head, fingers sinking into his dark hair. "Jilly, you should listen to Caleb," I said slowly, looking into her eyes. "If you know what's good for you."

The corners of her mouth bent towards her chin. She snatched Caleb's hand and pulled him away from me. She turned and started heading west, dragging him behind her. I followed—I couldn't help it. Caleb kept turning his head to me as she pulled him, looking at me with that same open-mouthed look.

I don't know what came over me. The hunger. My primal instincts. In that moment, cloaked in darkness, shielded by my entourage, everyone's attention back on the puppeteer, I decided to click my watch twice to turn off my camouflage. For just one moment, I showed the boy my true self.

He looked at me and his eyes widened with horror, before I changed back to my projected form. He began screaming manically, running and pulling Jilly along with him. She looked back at me with confusion and concern. I shrugged at her; my lips pressed into a tight smile. I watched the two until they disappeared into the warm night, then ordered Sylvia to call a car.

✦ ✦ ✦

Sylvia sat across from me in the car, blips of emotion streaking across her face. I wondered what could possibly be going on in her head. Not that I ever cared to ask.

"That crowd was enamored with you, ma'am," she said.

"Not enough," I said. I didn't have to worry about faking emotions around her.

She half-chuckled, tilting her head. "You have all the love in the world, ma'am."

Our car pulled up to the Governor's mansion.

"Go home, Sylvia."

"Yes, ma'am."

I got out and shut the door. The car drove Sylvia away and I entered alone.

I used to laugh at the interior of the home—that *this* is what they considered fancy—but now, it just added to the rotten feeling in my stomach.

I turned on lights in the foyer so that people knew I was home, but kept the rest of the lights in the house off. My eyes quickly adjusted to the darkness as I walked past the kitchen and into the bathroom. I thought of the puppet as I looked at the wrinkles under my eyes in the mirror. I unbuttoned my clothes, letting them fall to my ankles.

I pushed my cheeks up and smiled at the mirror. I tried it in a more exaggerated way, stretching my lips and squinting my eyes. I relaxed and let an easy smile rest under my nose like it had always been there. I disabled my camouflage and took off my watch, the pink skin on my arm transforming to black scales.

My sagging pink breasts hardened into a singular mound across my chest, coated in smooth obsidian scales. My hair, ears, nose, and lips disappeared, and my pronounced lower jaw jutted forward. The white of my eyes changed to red and my pupils elongated.

I tried smiling, just as I had before, but my scaled face made no expression. I pushed up my cheeks and tried bending the edges of my lips. Nothing. My mouth opened and closed from the attempts. I gave up trying to see emotion in my face and ran my tongue along my serrated teeth, inspecting the gums. Done with the mirror, I walked away, stomping over my clothes.

I opened the basement door and skulked down the stairs. My lair. Metal tanks and a silver toolbox lined the wall at the bottom of the steps. I walked to the center of the otherwise empty room and stopped at the two-foot-diameter hole in the concrete. Dropping to my knees, I crawled into the hole, digging my claws in the soil. I twisted my whole body in the dirt and curled up, wrapping my tail up to my face. With a deep breath, I closed my eyes and thought of home.

"Jax," I heard in a guttural voice, as a red portal opened directly above me. I immediately sat straight and craned my neck up. Crisscrossed metal bars occupied the immediate foreground of the portal—as if to remind me where I was.

"*Beluut ut* Garr," I said telepathically.

Garr's scales looked redder than usual. Light from a fire flickered off the rock behind him and reflected in his eyes. He huffed through his slanted nostrils and spoke through his mouth. "I could add a decade to your sentence for attempting to speak to me in the sacred language."

I bowed my head. "May the Flying Serpent purify my sins in fire."

"You are unworthy."

"I am unworthy," I repeated.

"Your high-frequency camouflage image was manually disabled while outside a safe zone. What was the reason?"

I raised my head. "Technical difficulties. A camera flash blew out my left sensor and I had a fraction of a second to reboot the system." The one perk of being exiled from telepathic communication: lying was easier.

Garr sat idle for a moment. I could tell he was communicating telepathically with someone else, as the vertical-slit pupils in his yellow eyes tilted from side-to-side. "Were any cameras in view of the incident?"

"With certainty, I can assure there were no witnesses, camera or otherwise."

Another moment passed in which Garr blinked twice and said nothing. I could hear worms squirming through the soil. "For your sake, I hope you're correct. The Magistrate is more committed than ever to see that you serve the duties of your sentence."

"But, why?" I asked.

"I'm not going to remind you of your crimes," Garr growled.

I shook my head. "No, I mean, why did we have to poison the water supply? We can't eat the tainted meat."

"You're not supposed to be eating them," he said without hesitation. "You're supposed to be eating the clones."

My stomach audibly growled. "How do I get more? I could serve my sentence better if I wasn't always hungry. Or is that part of my punishment, too?"

Garr stalled for a moment. "Your previous meal should last you another earth rotation. A clone will fill your incubator at that time."

"That's one per month. These clones lack nourishment," I snapped. "I need real food."

"Any more questions?" he prompted.

My hunger struck deep in the pit of my gut. I knew only one thing would get his attention.

"I want to get rid of someone," I said.

"A threat to your operation?" he asked.

"I think so."

"A reporter?"

"Worse," I said, and Garr leaned in. "An artist."

"Goodbye, Jax," he said, but I interrupted him.

"Sylvia said she sees the street performer outside the Capitol every day mocking me, and the crowd always laughs."

"Spoken like a true heiress. You bear no right to respect. Sylvia is a clone; she has no soul and no thoughts of her own. You have sixteen-thousand, eight-hundred and nineteen earth rotations remaining on your sentence. If you wish to return to your birthright, you will serve it without error and the Magistrate may see it reduced. If I have to contact you again like this... well, we will see."

The portal closed and a sickness growled in my stomach, aching to my core. I climbed out of the hole and ran to the bathroom, just in time to retch watery green bile into the sink. In the mirror, my black scales looked emaciated, graying around their edges. My red eyes had faded a dull orange. My body was rejecting this place. The sunlight. The food. I'd eaten fifty clones so far, each one less filling than the last. I couldn't take it any longer.

I picked up my watch from the bathroom counter. It was a bulky metal thing, with a cosmetic clock face on the front. I took it to the basement and snapped open the inner compartment. From within, I pulled a single strand of dark hair.

It would be illegal to replace the DNA sample within the internal construction of the incubator to create a more palatable clone. It would be, but it's only a crime if you get caught.

◆ ◆ ◆

In the morning, I returned to my office, but my thoughts were moving too quick to focus on anything. I stood in a front room at the top of the Capitol building, looking out the window. It was an empty office, and it struck me that I had never been in this room before, but it provided the perfect view of the government plaza below. The puppeteer was there in the same spot, entertaining a small crowd. The blooming sun reflecting off of everything gave me a headache, so I put on thick black sunglasses to continue watching.

My stomach growled at me and I had to look away. Curiosity drew me back to the window. This kept happening. I examined the whole space: a garden with cosmetic boulders on the right side of the plaza, carts and stands selling miscellaneous goods to the left, and straight across, the terrace bustling with pedestrians. I examined each human that strolled by, but from here, I couldn't smell anything.

"Governor Valentine, do you need something?" Sylvia asked in the door frame. I couldn't answer truthfully, so I said no. She said I had a press conference late that evening.

"I'm not feeling well, I can't make it," I said. I could hear her jot something down in her notes. "Don't cancel it, though."

"Is everything alright, ma'am?" she said. I turned and examined her eyes, sliding the sunglasses off my face. I wondered if it was true that she had no consciousness of her own.

"What do you think happens to you when you die?" I asked her.

"Excuse me?" she said.

"It's okay, take your time to think about it."

"Well, ma'am, I believe that when I die, my soul will go to heaven and I'll be reunited with all my relatives."

My lips curled into a half smile. I brushed the orange hair from her shoulder and placed my hand there, looking deeply into her bright blue eyes.

"I look forward to being reunited with mine, as well. We all need hope." I walked past her into the elevator. She followed me. I hit the third floor button to my office.

"Take the rest of the day off," I told her. "Go be happy while you still can."

She gave me a confused look, squinting her eyes, but responded, "Yes, ma'am."

The elevator dinged. I exited and Sylvia stayed, as the doors closed.

After locking my office door, I opened the windows and sat at my desk. I clasped my hands and sat perfectly still for hours. Stilling my physical body, as to quicken my mind. I didn't feel hungry anymore. The pangs that used to pierce my gut with pain now filled my mind with lucidity, waves of clear-headed inertia accelerating.

Just as the sun set, I unclasped my hands, stood and left. Nodding to the security guard on my way out, I stepped into the twilight.

The government plaza was nearly empty, yet the puppeteer still stood out by the terrace, performing for no one. I navigated the shadows to the garden on the right and slid up against the boulder.

Feeling the porous texture under my skin, still warm from the sun, reminded me of home.

I inhaled deeply to smell the filth of any humans. The coast was clear, and the bushes provided decent coverage. I took off my watch and my camouflage nullified. Not technically disabled.

My fingernails changed to claws and I used them to dig a hole into the garden. I dug as deep as I could go, trying to be as undisruptive to the plants as possible. As I clasped handfuls of soil and moved them to the side, I shimmied myself into the hole. My day clothes were getting filthy, but I didn't care. Ducking my head, I pushed dirt back into the hole, trying to smooth out the outer surface. I pulled my arm in, leaving a tiny gap for air at the top.

With a deep breath, I stilled my body, trying to sense any movement. With my body curled, nostrils facing the surface, I waited. In an hour, people began arriving for my press conference. The tainted scents of sweaty meat bags wafted around me, their garbled sounds echoing off the boulder. I snapped out of my trance as my nose detected the sweetest meaty smell. And one particularly horrible one.

Undeniably, the scent of Jilly and Caleb had returned. I wondered what kind of parents would let those two out alone at night. And then I thanked them.

Eventually, the press figured out there would be no conference, and their smells wafted away. The chlorinated cigarette smoke remained persistent.

Bowing my head and going still, I closed my eyes and raised my consciousness from my skull. I peered around the garden, past the boulder, and spotted the duo by the puppeteer.

"I don't want to be here anymore," Caleb whined.

"Just stay right here," Jilly ordered. "I'll be back soon."

I pressed towards her in astral mode and tried entering through her frizzy head.

"I promise, and then I'll take you to get ice cream after," she said. I saw Caleb through her eyes, frowning, on the verge of tears. "You didn't see anything last time, it was just your imagination."

Caleb mumbled a response and she left him. She walked up the steps to the Capitol, which is when I took over. I walked her to the top of the steps and through the front door. I looked at the guard at the front desk.

"Excuse me, sir, is there a bathroom I can use?" I made her ask.

"Right around the corner," he said, pointing.

"Thank you," I said through her, and walked her into the bathroom, locking her in a stall. Then I disabled her motor functions.

I snapped back to my body in the dirt, covered in soiled clothes. Closing my eyes, I raised my consciousness from the garden once again. Caleb had his chin on his knees, pouting as he watched the puppeteer. He was the only one watching. The puppet version of myself was trying to cheer him up, to no avail. He would soon feel much better.

My consciousness entered his head and I looked at the puppet through his eyes. It was doing something stupid to try to make Caleb laugh. I looked up to the gray-haired man and scrunched Caleb's face.

"You talentless bag of bones," I made Caleb say. The puppeteer did a double-take, surprised. "If you actually want to try something artistic and entertaining, you should jump off this terrace right now and kill yourself."

"Hey, kid, watch your mouth," shouted the puppeteer.

"Watch this," I said through Caleb, raising his middle finger, and making him walk away. I walked him to the garden, stood him next to the boulder, and disabled his motor functions.

The tantalizing smells of tender meat were so close as I snapped back to my body. I found my watch and placed it on my wrist. My scales changed back to wrinkled flesh with delicate fingernails and I carefully pulled myself out of the dirt. Patting the dirt off my clothes, I saw Caleb standing there with his mouth agape. I couldn't wait any longer.

"Are you a vampire?" Caleb asked. I gasped, shocked that he could speak, but figured his body built a tolerance to the paralysis from last time. I chuckled at his question. Sliding my hand along the boulder, I slowly stepped towards him.

"Myths are always easier to believe than the truth," I said. He didn't move at all and gave no response.

"Are you alright over there?" called the puppeteer to Caleb. "Hello?"

Annoyed, I leaned against the boulder and placed my consciousness into Caleb's head. Turning him around, I made him say, "Could you mind your own business for once. Leave me alone."

"Alright, I tried," responded the man. I exited Caleb without turning him back around.

Looking across the plaza, I saw it to be completely empty, save for the puppeteer, who was packing his things. The moment had arrived, and I wasn't going to waste it.

Without disabling my camouflage, I unhinged my lower jaw, and with a pop, felt it go slack against my breast. I placed my hands on Caleb's shoulders, as I unhinged my upper jaw and my eyes sat at the top of my head towards the stars. I bent forward and swallowed his body whole, clothes and all, leaning all the way to the ground. I stood, open jaw to the sky, two feet sticking out, and I removed the red shoes from his feet. I shoved his feet further in, clicking both jaws back into place, and closed my mouth.

My eyes came back over the top of my head and, as I focused, I saw the puppeteer completely frozen, a horrified silent scream stuck on his face. I smiled a big smile, one I genuinely felt for the first time. And just like that, he unfroze.

Arms wailing, dropping his things, he backed away, a piercing shriek bellowing from his withered face. He tripped, stumbling onto the stone railing of the terrace, and the last I saw of him was his legs, sliding over the edge. His panicked screams continued all the way to the bottom and then stopped with a splash.

I fell back into the dirt, satiated in a way I hadn't felt in years. Releasing my consciousness from my skull, I retrieved Jilly from the bathroom stall, making her thank the guard on her way out. I left her in front of the Capitol building and snapped back to my physical body.

My smile beaming, I stood and walked from the plaza toward the street, still carrying a small pair of red shoes. With a full stomach, I felt like nothing could bring me down. I called a car, eager to retrieve the clone waiting in my incubator.

✦ ✦ ✦

"The independent investigation has reached its conclusion," I said to the reporters outside the Capitol, still satiated from my meal three weeks before. Garr had yet to contact me again.

Jilly stood among the reporters with a serious look on her face. I pressed my lips and furrowed my brow.

"I must apologize, because I now know the wrong-doing came directly from my office. The decision to switch the water supply was made by Sylvia Vernon without my knowledge, and she has been arrested." Gasps came from the audience and cameras flashed.

"There is nothing I can do to change the past, but now we can all work together and look forward to a brighter future."

"There will be no questions," said my new assistant. All the reporters dutifully began packing up. Except one.

Jilly stepped forward, camera phone held out in her hand.

"You know something that you're not telling us," she said. "I know you're up to no good."

"The matter has been resolved," I said with a shrug and started walking away.

"This isn't over," she shouted, trying to follow me.

I stopped as I noticed a pair of red shoes running towards her. My new Caleb looked exactly the same, but didn't smell as delicious. He grabbed Jilly's hand from behind, looking up to me with a blank expression. He waved as she grimaced. I waved back, smiling for the camera.

James P. W. Martin is a storyteller of many mediums and genres. With a degree in Film Production from Emerson College, he works as a video editor, crafting stories for documentaries and TV series, as well as comedic YouTube videos, such as his Cat Broadcast Station series. His self-produced short films have been showcased in film festivals across the country. He writes screenplays, satire, politics, and reviews for The Boundary-Bending Blog, aptly named for his provoking, genre-defying style. James lives in Bucks County, Pennsylvania where you just might be lucky enough to catch him killing it at karaoke. He is honored to be published among such talented writers and has big plans for his own collection of short stories and future novels.

16

THE LAST PAGE

Hey, it's Rhea the Rebel, and you're listening to Radio 204.9 WWIZ. Just a heads-up if you were planning on heading downtown, you may want to take a raincheck. Our girl Gwendolyn Godfrey and her followers are currently locked in battle with the nefarious Prime Minister Ogg. As you well know, unless you've just recently awoken from a sleeping curse, it was Gwendolyn Godfrey who exposed Prime Minister Ogg's evil plan to enslave the wizard population using her unlikely and seemingly useless power to summon frogs. Knowing Ogg, this battle will be a bloody one."

I shake my head and a rogue strand of raven black hair settles irritatingly across it and into my line of vision. I let out a deep breath, blowing the errant strand against the side of my head where it belongs. Clutching the microphone, I drudge up as much enthusiasm as I can muster.

"In lighter news, the Witches Research Consortium for Health and Regulation has concocted a potion that removes acne, leaving perfect unblemished skin. The potion known as Skin Be New hits shelves next week. But let's keep this day rocking. Up next, 'Love In A Cauldron' by The Wicked Witchlets."

Mechanically, I reach out, nudging the stylus so that it rests against the record.

"*Mmhmm yeah. Eye of newt, tongue of man, gypsum root, and oleander,*

Different as they may be all meld together harmoniously in the cauldron."

The lead singer's voice croons as I flick off my mic. I grab the open bottle of ale by the neck and take a swig. The Wicked Witchlets dropped their new single last week (or eight pages ago), and I'm already sick of the idiotic lyrics. I've heard it so many times that the opening chords set my head to pounding. But running this radio station is the curse I chose. The second real choice I ever made. The first was choosing a name.

I started this station just over a year ago, or more precisely in Chapter Three, back when Gwendolyn could barely summon a tadpole, let alone an army of frogs. The Author, in a cruel act of egotistical omnipotence, decided to imbue me with self-awareness. Me, an un-named background character, offering to tell fortunes in the mid-city bazaar. Just one line in this monotonous droning narrative is dedicated to my existence, and She only wrote me in to create a more immersive atmosphere for the reader. A minor detail to add a bit of flair.

I run my hand absently over my crystal ball though I know full well it holds no secrets—old habits die hard even when you're fictitious. Besides, the smooth glass feels comforting against my gnarled hands. Gnarled! You heard, right. She writes one damn line about me, and it just *had* to include gnarled hands.

"Love in a Cauldron-dron-dron..."

Whittling my lower lip with my teeth hard enough to draw blood, I flip up the stylus and switch on my mic.

"Sorry about that, folks, skipping records are always a risk in the radio biz." Lovingly—the repetitive beat may drive me crazy, but I respect the magic of music—I slip the record back into its sleeve.

"Want to request a song or know a jinx to prevent records from skipping? Call in now." I drum my fingers against the desk, leaving oily smudges in their wake. A little light flashes on the console, indicating a caller on line one.

"Hey, you're on the air with Rhea the Rebel. What's your name?" I say, cringing at the sound of my voice, which drips with disingenuous cheer.

A raspy voice echoes through the speaker. "Barra Bell. I listen to your station all the time."

A bit of real warmth creeps into my voice. "Well, Barra, it's always nice to hear from an avid listener. What song would you like to request?"

"Oh, I don't want to request a song. I need some advice."

I lean eagerly into the mic, splaying my fingers against the desk. As a fortune-teller, I'm in my element when giving advice. "Well, I do give rather good advice. Lay it on me."

"Downtown is getting pretty hectic. So, I guess I was wondering what we do if Gwendolyn doesn't win?"

"Now, that's no way to think," I say with far more optimism than I feel. "Besides, we all know how these battles go. Gwen narrowly defeats Ogg, who somehow manages to get away. Just stay out of the blast zone, and you'll be a-okay. Thanks for calling in Barra!"

"But—" Barra blurts out before I hang up and patch through the next caller.

"Next caller. Hi, you're on the air with Rhea the Rebel. What's your name?"

"Sara, Sara Neighed."

Author, these names. You know what? I'm glad the Author didn't bother to name me. Rhea the Rebel may not be the most beautiful name, but it certainly beats a poorly written pun.

"Well, Sara Neighed, what song can I serenade you with?"

"Forget music, Rhea. Things are really dicey out here. I mean, Prime Minister Ogg conjured a massive blood serpent. Like it's a huge, writhing, sanguine mass of destruction!"

"Yes, well," I begin.

"And Gwendolyn summoned a tornado of frogs to battle it! I mean, honestly, I get that she's the hero, but does she realize that her frog spawn are wreaking just as much havoc as Ogg's sanguine serpent?"

"Sara, I'm sure she—"

"I mean, they're destroying the city! Surely, we should evacuate, but where to go? Where will we be safe from this chaos?" Her voice rises in a trembling crescendo.

"The battle between good and evil can be a terrifying thing to witness," I say in as soothing a tone as I can manage. "But I assure you, Sara, and those listening in tonight, there is nothing to fear. Gwendolyn Godfrey will come out on top." I hold back a sigh as I tap the End Call button.

The console lights blink out a spastic Morse code. I rub my temples as if I can soothe away the mounting pressure in my skull. Sure, the Author has time to write in an anti-pimple potion, but I suppose a jinx to cure migraines just didn't make the cut. Deliberately ignoring my incoming calls, I pull my wand from where it rests above my ear and make a swishing motion. A record flies off the shelf and lands gracefully on the record player.

"Okay, my witches and wizards, my goblins and gnomes, let's keep this party going. Here's an oldie by Van Howling that's sure to have you dancing like a beast."

I flick the stylus down, switch off the mic, and lean back in my blush-pink velvet chair.

"A-ooh. When the moon is full, and you feel the need to get on all fours and dance like a beast."

My head begins to pound in earnest. I bring my bottle of ale against my lips. Empty, damn. I tilt my head back and manage to down a few drops that were clinging to the sides. Truthfully, it doesn't matter who wins. Whether Ogg drains Gwendolyn dry or she finally lands the killing blow. It doesn't matter because this is the climax, the last battle. At this point, we've got what, thirty pages left, tops? And then the story ends, and we likely end with it.

I bear this burden alone. Who will remember the nameless urchin boy, all skin and bones, dirt caching his ruddy cheeks once the last page is turned? Who will think fondly of the precocious young chamber maid who took pity on Gwendolyn in Chapter Two, once our tale ceases to be told? What happens to us creatures of imagination when left to rot on a dusty shelf?

I wave my wand once more, summoning a bottle of sweet wine. A second flick of the wrist sends the cork popping. The taste of elderberry and peach is welcoming on my tongue. Thank the Author that She thought to write in a thriving brewery and winery. I don't know how I would have made it through the last two-hundred pages without the sweet tickle of giggle juice to calm my nerves.

"*Aah-ooh-ooh-ooh, DANCE LIKE A BEAST!*"

The lead singer shrieks the last line, which feels like a hammer pounding against the inside of my skull. I grit my teeth and summon another record off the shelf.

"I'm Rhea the Rebel, and you're listening to Radio 204.9 WWIZ. That was 'Dance Like A Beast' by *Van Howling*," I say, flicking on the mic and doing my best not to slur my words.

"Up next is The Wand Breakers with—" Shit. The console's lighting up like a fireworks display. Each flash is like a dagger to the eye.

"On second thought, it looks like we've got some callers waiting. Let's chat it up, shall we? Hi, you're on the air with Rhea the Rebel. What's your name?"

"This is Hollow Graham," a reedy voice answers.

Is She kidding me right now? And I thought Sara Neighed was bad.

"Well, Hollow, if you're worried about the battle downtown, I can assure you there's nothing to fear." My voice sounds steady, authoritative. I'd pat myself on the back if I wasn't worried I'd topple out of my chair. The room is wobbly. I'm not sure if it's due to my migraine or all the alcohol I've consumed.

"But Rhea, the battle's over! Gwendolyn won! It's over!" Hollow keeps talking, but I can't seem to make out the words. There's a low hum in my ears, and my stomach seems to have curled in on itself. So, this is it then.

"Isn't it amazing? Rhea?"

The sound of my name snaps me back to reality. "Yes, yes, truly wonderful. Well, it was great to hear from you, Hollow."

My heart slams ferociously against my chest as I end the call. I frown down at the console. The lines are flooded with callers, each wanting to comment on Gwendolyn's victory. I should patch them through, let them use their voices while they still have them. But I don't.

"It sounds like we've reason to celebrate. So, let's break at that pop-punk favorite 'Try'n Jinx Me Now' by The Hatter Was Sane All Along.

I switch out the record. My gnarled hands shake as I flick the stylus into place.

"Go ahead, whoo-hoo, try and jinx me now."

I can't help but stare at my hands, which I have long resented. They're wrinkled well beyond my years, the skin hanging loose over bone and sinew. Soon they'll be gone just like the rest of me. Will we be aware of it when it happens, or will we fade away too quickly for conscious thought? Author, I hope it's quick.

The song ends, and I switch it out with a random record, not bothering to announce the tune. Let them dance in the streets; let them celebrate while they can. These people, my people whom I've tried so hard to protect. I cannot stop the book from closing but at least I have spared them the knowledge.

It's over, and we've got what minutes, pages? No, paragraphs until we're not but bone-dry ink tattooed on pulpy parchment. I grab the wine bottle. Bringing it to my mouth, I inhale the sweet summery scent before letting it spill between my lips. This will be the last thing I ever taste. The thought chills my insides, and suddenly, the wine tastes far too sweet. The bottle slips from betwixt my gnarled fingers, and I numbly watch it shatter. On any other page, I'd make a great fuss, clean up the shards and curse myself under my breath. But here on the last page, I can't seem to find any reason to make the effort.

I reach for my crystal ball, cupping it in my hands. Like a child with a plush toy, I hold it tight against my chest, resting my cheek against its smooth surface. It comforts me, and I feel my breath even out. Panicking changes nothing. I look around the cramped room at the shelves cluttered with vinyl and liquor bottles. A light breeze drifts in through the open window. Did She write that breeze just for me? Or does it, too, have a mind of its own? I lick my swollen lips; they taste like wine. Another song ends, and I switch on my mic. It takes a moment to find my voice as if it is fading from me.

"Hello, my vampires and werewolves, my pixies and ghosts. This is Rhea the Rebel and you're listening…"

❖ ❖ ❖

Scarlet Wyvern is part poet, part girl, and part dragon. Since she was a young hatchling, Scarlet has reveled in the written word. Wyvern is fascinated by mythology, especially that which concerns the fair folk and is utterly obsessed with the original Grimm fairy tales. When she is not busy writing or soaring through the sky lighting villages on fire, Wyvern delights in reading, photography, playing video games, singing karaoke and making snarky comments while sipping the blood of her enemies out of a crystal chalice. To learn more visit ScarletWyvern.com or follow @ScarletWyvern on Twitter.

ABOUT THE PRESS

Our mission at Dandelion Revolution Press (DRP) is to write and publish the female forward stories we want to read. No matter how our authors identify, we celebrate diverse women characters and explore their impact on society. DRP was founded in 2019 by four women from the Greater Philadelphia area—Bethany Chernay, Ashini J. Desai, Hayley E. Frerichs, and Paige Gardner. They serve as the current editors alongside guest editors Scarlet Wyvern and Swapna Padhye. Learn more at DandelionRevolutionPress.com and follow their journey on Twitter @DandelionPress.